Editor: Talia Leduc
All rights reserved.
ISBN-13: 978-1998775323

Give feedback on the book at:
lorhainneeckhart@hotmail.com

Twitter: @LEckhart
Facebook: AuthorLorhainneEckhart

Printed in the U.S.A

Fallen Hero

THE FRIESSEN LEGACY

THE OUTSIDER SERIES
BOOK THREE

LORHAINNE ECKHART

The Friessen Family Series
Reading order:

The Outsider Series

The Forgotten Child (Brad and Emily)
A Baby And A Wedding
Fallen Hero (Andy, Jed, and Diana)
The Search
The Awakening (Andy and Laura)
Secrets (Jed and Diana)
Runaway (Andy and Laura)
Overdue
The Unexpected Storm (Neil and Candy)
The Wedding (Neil and Candy)

The Friessens: A New Beginning

The Deadline (Andy and Laura)
The Price to Love (Neil and Candy)
A Different Kind of Love (Brad and Emily)
A Vow of Love, A Friessen Family Christmas

The Friessens

The Reunion
The Bloodline (Andy & Laura)
The Promise (Diana & Jed)
The Business Plan (Neil & Candy)
The Decision (Brad & Emily)
First Love (Katy)
Family First
Leave the Light On
In the Moment
In the Family: A Friessen Family Christmas
In the Silence
In the Stars
In the Charm
Unexpected Consequences
It Was Always You
The First Time I Saw You
Welcome to My Arms
Welcome to Boston (A Paige & Morgan Short Story)
I'll Always Love You
Ground Rules
A Reason to Breathe
You Are My Everything
Anything For You
The Homecoming
When They Were Young (Link included FREE with
The Homecoming)
Stay Away From My Daughter
The Bad Boy
A Place of Our Own
The Visitor

All About Devon
Long Past Dawn
How to Heal a Heart
Keep Me In Your Heart

The Friessen Family

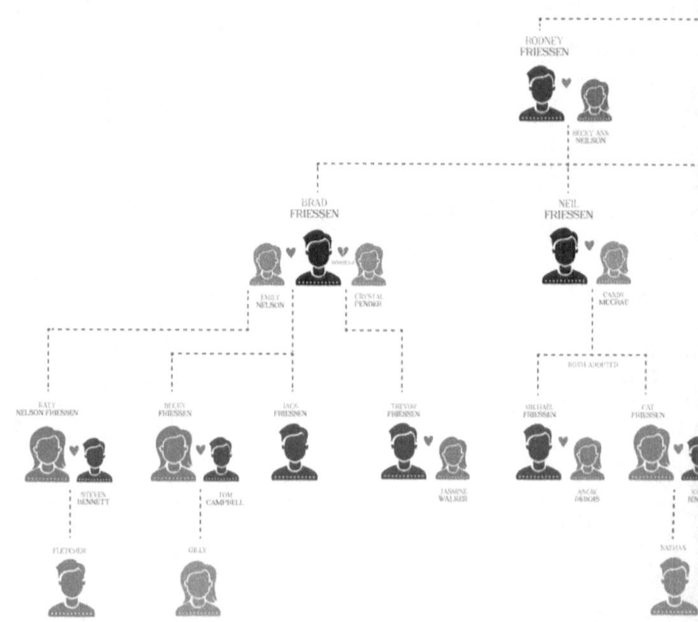

The Outsider Series

THE FORGOTTEN CHILD	BRAD & EMILY
A BABY AND A WEDDING	BRAD & EMILY & Rodney & Becky
FALLEN HERO	JED, DIANA & ANDY
THE SEARCH	JED, DIANA & ANDY
THE AWAKENING	ANDY & LAURA

The Outsider Series

SECRETS	DIANA & JED *with the entire Friessen Family*
RUNAWAY	ANDY & LAURA
OVERDUE	JED & DIANA
THE UNEXPECTED STORM	NEIL & CANDY
THE WEDDING	NEIL & CANDY *and the entire Friessen Family*

The Friessens: A New Beginning

THE DEADLINE	ANDY & LAURA
THE PRICE TO LOVE	NEIL & CANDY
A DIFFERENT KIND OF LOVE	BRAD & EMILY
A VOW OF LOVE	THE ENTIRE
A FRIESSEN FAMILY CHRISTMAS	FRIESSEN FAMILY

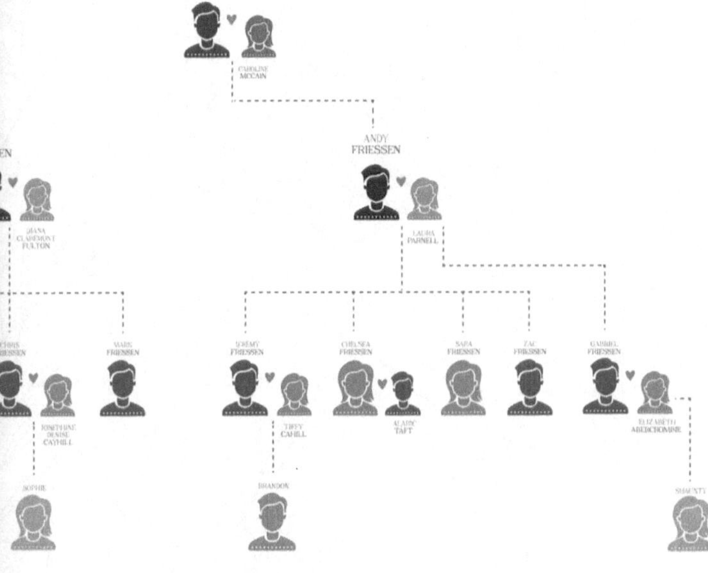

The Friessens

The Friessens

—Another great book in this series and by this author. I am going to start reading *The Awakening* right after I am done with this review; I cannot wait!

– PAULA

—When life deals an innocent a bad hand, it isn't surprising when they want revenge. This story handles the situation in a simple fashion. Turning anger and distrust into love. Well written, and a story which leaves you wanting to read more about this family.

– VORACIOUS READER

—Deals with some social issues but never strays from taking a chance on love and overcoming insurmountable issues and losses to let the heroine find and claim true love against all odds.

– BILLIE MILLER

A love story of unexpected second chances.

Diana Fulton, a young lawyer, has returned to her hometown in search of revenge, never having forgotten how she was treated as a child, tossed into the system after she and her sister became collateral in a game between two powerful men, all because of the secrets and lies of her mother.

For fifteen years, she has remembered the Friessen

name, the name of her tormentors. Despite the difficult hand she was dealt, she's planned for the day she could exact revenge. The only problem is that nothing is simple and easy, especially when it comes to getting even. When she lands on the doorstep of Jed Friessen at his rundown ranch, she finds a man who is nothing like his cousin or uncle, and she begins to question everything she once believed.

In fact, Jed shows her kindness, compassion, and something else she didn't believe possible: that a man could truly have her back. But the feelings of anger and distrust that have driven her for so long are filled with a promise she made to herself and her sister. Can Diana put aside her hate to see that the thing she hasn't known she's been looking for all her life is standing right in front of her? A man who loves a woman will do anything for her, but she needs to take a chance on love.

CHAPTER
One

Diana pushed aside the creamy lace curtain that fluttered in the breeze and gazed out on a yard adorned in pinks and frothy whites, with ribbons and bows and more flowers than she'd ever seen. The midday sun had turned the sky a deep blue over miles of open land. To Diana, this was paradise. Several long tables were draped with lacy white cloth, glasses stacked in pyramids. The waiters wore white shirts, and what she thought were a hundred wedding guests were all dressed in their Sunday best. Rows of white chairs faced a beautiful arbor covered with pink and white roses, with baby's breath woven through the chain of flowers, a spectacular sight. Everyone was there: her groom, his family, and his friends in North Lakewood. But there would be no family there for Diana, and no father to give her away.

She let the antique lace curtain fall and stepped away from the window when her soon-to-be husband glanced up at her from the yard. The love in his eyes for her had never failed to take her breath away, and she had to remind herself where she'd come from. This wasn't a dream but was so very real. That she would come back to North Lakewood had been a promise she made to herself, one of anger, one of retribution, one of justice, but she'd never imagined she'd find love or learn that there existed, in fact, men who were truly honorable, courageous. This man was her hero, who loved her so deeply and understood who she truly was. As she remembered what she'd survived, Diana knew what didn't kill her had only made her stronger.

She would soon be Mrs. Friessen, marrying a man she knew would fight all her battles for her if she let him. He was a proud, strong man who would always have her back and always protect her, and maybe that was why she had to remind herself again that this was real.

She glanced in the antique mirror one last time. Tracing her finger under her eye, she wiped away a tear she hadn't realized she'd shed, not of sadness but joy, the kind she'd never believed she'd feel. Her makeup was perfect, and as she took in her vivid blue eyes, she no longer saw the terrified, angry girl filled with such disillusionment and hate. Her fiery red hair was combed and pinned up in cascading curls, a shimmering white veil with roses fastened to the back. She smoothed the chiffon of her wedding dress down, feeling the tightness in her chest, again reminding herself this was real, when a soft knock on the bedroom door interrupted the thoughts she'd been left with for far too long.

She turned to the closed door, hearing voices and laughter outside.

"Diana, are you ready?"

She pulled in a breath and nodded to herself in the

mirror as the door opened and a woman she barely knew offered her a kind smile before walking over to her, holding out a lovely bouquet of pink and white roses. Diana reached for it, feeling the joy and love.

"Everyone is waiting, I see," Diana said. She took in the gorgeous bouquet as she turned back to the mirror and her image, again breathing in the scent of roses.

"They are. Are you ready?"

She made herself take another breath, shutting her eyes for a second, imagining where she'd come from. Then she turned, her skirt rustling, and felt a smile touch her lips from the joy she couldn't hold back. "Yes, I'm more than ready," she said. "I've been waiting my whole life for this moment."

Diana Claremont had been born thirteen years ago in a county hospital that had long since burned down. She had a mother, a baby sister, and no middle name. She'd asked her mother only once why she didn't have one, as all the kids at school did, and her only response was "Don't be ridiculous." She had a name: Diana. There was no reason for a middle name that would never be used. Diana's mother, Faye Claremont, wasn't the kind of woman who cared what others thought. She didn't spend time with her daughters, baking cookies or tucking them into bed, and she didn't give a damn what they were thinking or feeling or whether they followed the rules society laid out.

From her earliest memory, it seemed Diana had always looked after herself and stayed out of Faye's way. She was grateful the fall days were still warm enough that she could run barefoot down to the creek, exploring the thick forest behind her house and then lying in the long grass, dreaming of any life except her own. In those moments, she could believe in fairytales and princes and dashing knights on horses, hoping one day soon a prince would ride in and take her away from this life. Then she would open her eyes and breathe in the reality of empty cupboards, always guessing what mood her mother would be in, and a hollow ache inside she could never fill.

She sat up, feeling the pull of her frayed cutoffs and worn mud-brown t-shirt. She had scrawny legs and arms and thick, long red hair that she could never tame. She breathed in the sweet scent of the remaining fully ripe blackberries as she sat in the middle of a field under the bright sun and cloudless deep blue sky. Towering green treetops shaded the carpeted path that wound through the thick forest behind her house to that big open field. Paradise was where she could hide out, watching her four-year-old baby sister, Louisa, in a faded yellow dress, picking juicy plump berries and shoving them in her mouth.

Louisa didn't have her red hair, and her eyes were a different shade of blue, but then, Diana didn't know who Louisa's father was. For that matter, she didn't know who hers was, either. Her stomach rumbled, again wishing for something other than berries to fill the empty hole. But the milk in the fridge had gone bad, and she knew the Chinese leftovers in a carton were for her mother, who'd been fast asleep when they left, having stumbled in and passed out, drunk, after closing out the bar, Diana figured. She'd learned long ago never to wake her.

Diana knew before long they would have to go home. As the sun dipped lower, so did the fall coolness, but for a moment, Diana fantasized about something better, a happy mother who would offer a smile, who would be up in the morning to fix breakfast, say good morning, and maybe, just once, tell her how much she loved her and her sister. A mother who would be there for them, talking, listening, caring, instead of the disinterested Faye Claremont, whose many moods Diana had learned to navigate long ago.

"Louisa, come on, we have to go," Diana called out, brushing the grass from her cutoffs. She hurried over to her sister just as she shoved another berry in her mouth, the black juice staining her dress and her face. "Oh no, Louisa, Mama is going to be mad."

But she knew her sister didn't understand. She stared up at her with vacant eyes, a little girl who knew Diana's name and only a handful of words. Her mother called her stupid, but Diana knew it was something else. Her sister took pills every morning for seizures she'd had since she was a baby. Diana wondered whether that was why she screeched at times and couldn't be reasoned with. She reached for her hand and pulled her along, hurrying down the trail barefoot toward the older two-story cedar house with its sagging porch and rotted windows.

She hurried to the door. The old hardwood floor was splintered and worn here and there. Diana knew enough of her mother's moods to understand that one look at Louisa and the blackberry mess would have her ranting, furious. Messes were something her mother never wanted to clean up. The screen door squeaked, and so did the floor.

"Diana, where've you been, girl? Get supper started," was all her mama shouted from the only bathroom, which they all shared. "I'm meeting Mr. Friessen at the carriage house, so I have to get going now. You know I don't like to keep him waiting."

"Sorry, Mama," was all Diana said as she pulled Louisa over to the old double sink in the kitchen, where the porcelain was cracked and the faucet dripped. She turned on the tap and lifted her sister, very aware her mother was still in the bathroom, primping, putting makeup on just as she did every evening before she went out. She heard a clatter and knew she was likely curling her long deep red hair. Diana washed off the sticky blackberry juice from Louisa's hands and face, then reached for the worn old dishtowel by the sink and dried her.

She strode down the hall to the bathroom, where the door was ajar. Her mother was shadowing her sky-blue eyes and adding thick mascara. A rolled cigarette burned by the sink, and the smell of weed was thick in the air. Faye was already in a tight black skirt and four-inch heels. For a second, she flicked her gaze directly to Diana in the mirror. It was never lost on her how beautiful her mother was. At the same time, that one look told her that whatever mood her mother was in, it wasn't a happy one.

"You've been gone most of the day, Diana. You been up to something you shouldn't be?"

What was she supposed to say? "Just playing in the forest, picking berries…"

"Fine, fine," Faye said. "Listen, I'm going to be late. Todd Friessen is taking me to that new steakhouse, one of the best in town, and I've been dying to try it. He really does love to spoil me. You mark my words, Diana: A wealthy man like Todd Friessen is our ticket out of this hell. One day, I'll be his missus. I deserve that, and by God, I will have it. Being his wife will make me important in this town, and then I'll look down on all those cackling gossipy women who've trash-talked me behind my back and slammed the door in my face. Yes, sir, you can bet I'll have the last laugh on them when I'm married to a man who owns all Todd Friessen does. The power he has in this county will be mine. You mark my words! Okay, how do I look?"

Her mother didn't look at her but at the mirror. Diana had heard all the cruel, hurtful whispers and names. People called her mother trashy, from the wrong side of the tracks, and had even muttered that the apple didn't fall too far from the tree. Diana thought they had been talking about her looks, but she realized their words were meant to sting. She knew Todd Friessen had a wife and a meanness that could turn on a dime when he didn't get what he wanted. She'd heard too many times from the locals that Faye was his new plaything, not that she'd known what that was, though she'd heard enough from her mother's bedroom and the squeak of the bed springs to figure out what Mr. Friessen was doing with her before going home to his wife.

"You look great, Mama," she said. She knew her mother didn't want to hear anything else.

Faye looked down at her, letting her vivid blue eyes linger over her. "I saw you making eyes at young Andy when he showed up the other day with that bike for you. That was really kind of him to buy it. I hope you thanked him properly. I don't want Todd thinking you're ungrateful, you hear me? I see the way you look at Andy, all googly eyed. He's damn handsome, just like his father, graduating this year. I heard he's dating the mayor's daughter and is expected to marry her, too, so don't be setting your sights on him."

It was the slap that seemed to always come from her mother.

"He won some cowboy thing," Faye continued. "Todd was telling me about that. Young Andy has had his fun, playing around in the rodeo, but his father's got plans for him. He's letting him play around a bit before he sends him off to college and then gets him settled into politics. Maybe he'll be running the country one day. His son is sowing his wild oats, is all I told him…just like his father." She let out a sigh and then laughed.

Diana wanted to set her straight on so many things about Andy Friessen. "Andy is a rodeo star, Mama," she said. "He won the men's cutting challenge and all around. It was his second year winning it. He's really very good! And I didn't ask for the bike. I caught my pants in my bike chain, and Andy stopped when he saw. He said the chain was rusty and tried to fix it…"

The way her mother was staring down at her made Diana stop talking. The fact was that Andy had rescued her, freeing her pants, and even pulled open his toolbox in the back of his pickup and tried to fix the rusty chain on the old bike, someone's castoff. Then he'd tossed her bike in the back and driven her home. She hadn't shared that part with her mother. The day after, he'd driven up in his pickup with a brand-new red bike for her, and it was on that day, from his kindness, that she'd sworn she'd love him forever. She found herself looking for his pickup every day now and hoping for a glimpse of him.

"I do the best I can, Diana," Faye said. "I hope you didn't whine to him and ask for it. You get what you get and make do with it." For a moment, she thought her mother was mad at her, and she wished she hadn't mentioned Andy now.

"Of course I didn't," she said. "I told you, he just bought it for me. He's nice."

Her mother only nodded and made a face. "Damn good looking, too. Tall, dark, and handsome, just like his father. He's a catch and then some. Why, if I were ten years younger, I'd be showing young Andy a thing or two…" Her mother smiled at her image in the mirror and let out a soft laugh again.

The knot tightened in Diana's stomach. She wasn't a fool; she knew what her mother was suggesting.

"No, Andy is all Todd talks about, thinks about, has plans for," Faye said. "He says everything he does is for his son. But I see all the women who are chasing Andy down, hoping he'll notice them. Yes, he's a catch." She tapped the chipped old yellow bathroom counter with her hand. "Okay. I cleaned this bathroom up again, so you make sure Louisa stays out of my makeup. She was playing in here yesterday with my face cream and made a mess, and you know I don't like that, cleaning up a mess I don't have time to clean. Keep her out of here. Cook up some of those frozen burgers in the freezer for dinner. Pretty sure the bread is gone. You'll have to eat it without. Oh, damn! Forgot my necklace…" Her mother slapped a hand to her chest, her long nails painted deep red, and then hurried out of the bathroom. Diana listened to the click of her heels as she went up the old wooden stairs.

Diana walked back out to see her baby sister sitting on the floor, chewing a crayon. "No, no, Louisa…" she called out and ran over, barefoot, to take the yellow crayon and wipe the bits from her mouth. She reached for the only coloring book Louisa had, on the old coffee table that had come with the house, and opened it to a page that had barely been scribbled on. She put the crayon in her hand and said, "Color me a picture. Don't put it in your mouth."

"How do I look?" Faye called out from the stairs, where she teetered on dark red heels, now in a red skirt and a red sequined halter. Apparently, she had changed, as well. She really was beautiful.

"You look great, Mama," Diana said. Faye had a one-track mind when it came to men, and as of late, it was all about Todd Friessen.

"I'm leaving," Faye said. "Bye, darling. I'll be home when I'm home. Again, do not make a mess I have to clean up." She bent to brush a kiss on Diana's head and dashed out the door without a glance at Louisa.

Diana watched through the window as Faye hurried to her new Jeep, deep red, striking. She still didn't know where she'd gotten the money to buy it, considering there was never enough money for food, but she figured it had something to do with the pills she packaged up at the kitchen table. There were nights she'd been woken by her mother arriving home with people she didn't know. The booze flowed, and the drugs came out, along with music and carrying on into the wee hours of the morning.

As the Jeep backed out down the narrow, heavily treed driveway, Diana wondered what surprises she'd be in for tonight, strangers and partying or Todd Friessen in her mother's bedroom?

At the same time, as she stared at the dust, all that remained of her mother in the driveway, she wished Andy Friessen would once again drive in and check that she was okay, tell her the rumors of him dating the mayor's daughter weren't true. One day, just maybe, he'd come courting her and would take her away from all this, her hero. She may have been only thirteen, but there was something about Andy Friessen that made her swear she'd love him forever. And maybe, one day, she prayed, she would be his wife.

Three

Something shattered and clanked. Diana bolted upright in bed, listening to the familiar drunken cursing of her mother, feeling the chill from the cool fall night. She glanced at the bedside clock, which read 1:10 a.m.—early for Faye. Her mother made no effort to be quiet as she stumbled around, but then, she never did when she brought the party home.

Diana listened for another voice, another sound, as she slipped out of her warm bed. The temperature was dropping, and she shivered as she crept toward the old wooden stairs and stood at the top in her thin pajamas, expecting to see half a dozen people smoking and drinking. But she listened, and there was nothing, no one else. Maybe that was why a sigh of relief slipped past her lips as she started carefully down the stairs.

"Mama, you're home early," she said.

Faye wobbled on her spiked heels against the island of the dingy old kitchen. She reeked of cheap booze, and instead of cigarette smoke, Diana thought it was the familiar stench of weed, something else she wished she didn't know, that lingered in the air.

Her mother yanked open the old, rotted cupboards. They were mostly bare of food. "Where's that sister of yours?" she slurred.

Diana wanted to snap, *Asleep, of course, which is where I should be, as it's after midnight.* But that would earn her a cuff, as her mama never would stand for any back talk, so she bit her tongue and calmly said, "She's asleep, Mama. I put an extra blanket on her, as it's colder tonight. Do you know when the oil tank will get filled so we have heat?" That was another thing her mother hadn't done, and Diana was beginning to worry, as the nights were growing colder.

Her mother didn't turn around as she teetered on her heels. Her mascara had smudged under her eyes, and the way she looked at her, Diana often wondered whether she hated her. Faye waved her hand as if she didn't know or care about keeping them warm, or fed, or anything Diana figured a mother should want to do.

"Got other things on my mind, Diana. Always have some problem landing on my doorstep. You want to tell me who you've been talking to?"

There it was, that feeling as if the rug were about to be yanked out from under her. Her mother stared at her with a meanness that had always terrified her. Diana's stomach knotted again, and she couldn't get her tongue to move. This was the unpredictable mother she didn't understand, and she knew she was fishing for something.

"Cat got your tongue there, girl? That damn social worker came sniffing around today when you were at school, asking a whole lot of questions about Louisa, about you, looking around as if she had the idea I wasn't looking after you. Then she demanded to see your sister. You been talking to any of them counselors at school again, telling them things about me you shouldn't have been?"

Diana felt her face tingle as she struggled to think of what she might have said. She was always careful at school, never saying much any time they pulled her out of class, asking too many questions about her mother, about whether she talked to her father, where she lived, and whether her little sister had been seen by a doctor. Why did they focus in on her?

"You won't answer, girl?" Faye swayed and stumbled closer, most likely ready to strike.

"No, Mama, I haven't talked to anyone. You know how they are about you being a single mother. They're looking to dig something up, is all. I said nothing." There was also the fact that her mother had looked like a two-dollar hooker the few times she'd been called in to sign something for Diana at school.

Faye swayed again, obviously satisfied with what she'd said. The strap of her barely decent black sequined top was ripped, and her skirt was stained with something brown as she stumbled to the table and sank into an old wooden chair. Dropping her head on her arms, she burst into tears and screeched as if someone were trying to kill her. This was always the killer for Diana. She walked over to her mother and pressed a hand to her deep red hair, running it gently over the waves. Faye whimpered and turned toward her.

"Do you think I'm beautiful, baby? Do you think men still find me desirable?"

She knew what her mother wanted to hear, and it wasn't the truth. Damn, she didn't want to be talking to her mother about men. She was just a kid who knew too much of the darker sides of what went on between a man and a woman. All she'd ever wanted was a mother who was there for her and Louisa rather than looking for a man to latch on to and fix all her problems.

"Of course you are, Mama. Any man would be lucky to have you."

Faye smacked her hand away. Sitting up, she tossed her head back and snorted a deep, throaty laugh. Diana hated when her mama got like this. Her moods would swing high and low, worse when she was drinking, worse still when she popped pills or smoked or snorted whatever she could get her hands on. Tonight, Diana could tell she'd done a little of everything. She could see it in her face, her eyes. Unpredictable, dangerous, wild.

"Mama, are you hungry? There's leftover macaroni in the fridge. I can heat you up some."

"No, I don't want no dinner. I want something to drink. Where's the liquor?" Faye started to get up and staggered, losing her balance and dropping back on the chair. Her mother was so far gone, and soon she'd pass out. It was always the same. Diana tried to think now whether her mother had ever been sober for a meaningful length of time.

"Mama, I'll get it for you. You just sit there." Diana hurried to the open cupboard by the old fridge, which held half a bottle of gin, the bottle of pills her sister took every morning, and nothing else. The bottle of juice in there had been gone a week earlier. They needed groceries, food, but this wasn't the time to bring it up. She reached for a glass in the dish drain and put it down in front of her mother.

"You're a good girl, Diana, but that damn idiot sister

of yours is bringing trouble to my doorstep, having social workers sniffing around as if they really care about her. Stick her in some home with some pedophile and nobody would care. But not you. You always look after me. If it weren't for you, I'd pack up and leave. Yes, I would. Some days I wish I could just leave here and never look back. I never asked for this life."

Diana turned her head, blinking back tears. She didn't know what she'd do if her mother abandoned her, and she feared that one day, Faye wouldn't come home. And Louisa, so defenseless—she wondered if her little sister knew how much her mother hated her. Why had the social worker shown up? Every day she went to school, she left her sister alone with her mother, who it seemed had always been angry, a woman with a sixth sense for others' misery. She could never let her mother know how much she hurt her, or that cruel side of Faye would move in for the kill, saying even crueler things she'd never remember in the morning.

Diana asked herself again, like she did so often, why her mother couldn't love her. She closed the cupboards her mother had yanked open and listened as Faye refilled her glass and sighed, and she turned to see her downing the glass of gin straight and then pouring another. A few more minutes and then she could safely sneak away, as it wouldn't be long until her mother laid her head down on the table and passed out. At least tonight she could be thankful for one thing: There'd be no party.

CHAPTER
Four

The Monday morning sun had just topped the horizon, and where was her mother but passed out at the kitchen table? The sight was not unfamiliar. Diana had school today, and as she washed her face in the bathroom, she knew she had only another hour before she had to leave. But walking out the door and leaving her sister with her passed-out mother was something she couldn't do.

She had just run a brush through her tangled red hair when there was a pounding at the front door. For a moment, she didn't know what to do. Her heart hammered in her chest, and as she hurried out of the bathroom, barefoot in her faded blue pajamas, she cast a glance to her mother, who hadn't stirred, one hand around the glass, her head resting on the table, the empty bottle of gin on the floor.

The door shook. As the pounding continued, Diana was positive it would splinter. She hurried to slip the lock, and when she pulled it open, there was Andy

Friessen, tall, dark, and furious. He pushed past her, right into the house, without a word or a glance to her.

"What did you do to my father?" he shouted as he strode right over to her mother, who hadn't moved, and slapped both hands to the table so hard that the sound ricocheted like a shot right through Diana. She jumped, and her heart thudded again as she saw the anger staring down at her mother. For a moment, she feared he'd hurt her.

Faye groaned, and Diana shivered in the chill of the early morning and quietly closed the door. Andy kicked the chair her mother was in until she stirred and nearly fell out of it. "What the hell…?" Faye moaned, lifting her head, likely still drunk. The scent lingered from the bender she was well into.

"Diana?" Louisa whined from the top of the stairs. Of course, she was scared, but so was Diana, who watched her mother stumble out of the chair. Andy took a step around it, stalking toward her, the fury coming off him in waves.

Diana forced herself to swallow, hurried over to the stairs, and ran up them to Louisa, who was rubbing her eyes, standing in the yellow nightgown Diana had put her to bed in.

"I asked you a question, and you damn well better answer me!" Andy shouted.

Diana reached for Louisa, knowing she was shaking. She couldn't make out what her mother said as she carried Louisa back down the stairs.

"My dad always comes home," Andy said. "But we had to search for him all night before we found him this morning at the carriage house, out cold—and it wasn't booze, Faye. I know damn well what he does with you there. You cheap slut, what did you do to him?"

Faye was cowering against the wall in the kitchen. Dark black circles coated her eyes from her cheap mascara. Louisa gripped Diana's thin pajama top, but she couldn't pull her gaze. Her heart was hammering in her chest. She'd never seen this side of Andy Friessen, a side that terrified her.

"I wasn't with him last night," Faye said. "Whatever happened, it wasn't me. He never showed up where he was supposed to. I came home early and was here all night. You know Todd's got a stable of women he beds regularly. It's not just me. When he tires of one, you know he finds a new favorite. He sleeps with half the county."

Diana always knew when her mother was lying. It had been late when she stumbled in drunk, and she had carried on about meeting Mr. Friessen at the carriage house, a cottage half a mile from there. Diana had never been inside, but she knew it was on the Friessen land, just like their house.

"You're a liar," Andy said. "Everyone knows you were with him. Everyone knows you're always at the carriage house, stashing dope, selling it, doing things you shouldn't. That Jeep you drive isn't exactly unnoticeable. Lying is exactly what I won't tolerate! My father's ignored it for a long time, but whatever you did last night, you went too far. You're a dangerous woman, Faye. Look at you. You stink of drugs, booze…" Andy stopped talking, and Diana watched as he dragged his gaze past her mother, taking in the old kitchen, the closed cupboards. She feared what he was thinking. "You may live here because of my father's generosity, but you're evil, Faye. This piece-of-shit house is here only because my father hasn't had it torn down. He should. You entice every decent guy in this county with your whoring around. I know my father isn't a saint, but damn you, Faye, and your bastards. You're an absolute stain on this community."

Diana realized she had gasped. She'd never heard such hatred from Andy. He must have heard her, because he leveled his hard, icy blue eyes on her, flashing with disdain, and said, "What time did Faye get home?"

She realized he was talking to her. From the tone of his voice, she could feel the demand, the anger, the hatred. What the hell was she supposed to say? She looked over to her mother, whose face was as white as a ghost, staring at her in a way that had her taking another step back, still holding her sister.

"Around midnight, I guess, give or take," she said.

Faye stumbled over to her, barefoot, and smacked her across the side of the head, just missing Louisa, whose scrawny arms were wrapped around her neck. "You lie, girl! Don't you listen to her, son. She's always lying."

Louisa screeched and buried her head against Diana's shoulder. Her legs were wrapped around her waist, and Diana felt tears streaming down her face, past the sting from her mother's hand, the shame and humiliation almost too much.

Andy did nothing, and the way he let his gaze linger on her, so unfeeling, before looking back to Faye hurt more than anything. "Yeah, well, that's what Claremonts do, isn't it? Lie. Like mother, like daughter. Is that what you teach your kids?" He glanced at the empty bottle on the floor and kicked it so it clattered against the wall, then flicked his gaze to Faye again. "Listen up, Faye! I'm done with the lies. You've gone too far this time. I'm giving you until nightfall to get the hell off this property. You disgust me, the whoring, the partying, the drugs. Everyone in this county knows what you deal here. I told my dad to toss you out long ago. You're not doing this on our land anymore, you hear me?"

Diana's stomach bottomed out, and her heart thudded. She pulled Louisa closer to her.

"You can't do that!" Faye yelled. "I've paid my rent, and there are laws to protect us. Your daddy will never agree."

"Protect you? You've never paid one dime in rent, Faye. Whatever my father was thinking, letting you stay here, I guarantee he's now come to his senses." He let out a rough laugh. "This is my family's land, just another piece-of-shit old house that should've been burned down long ago. You have no rights here. I just need to make one call to the sheriff and tell him about your pills, drugs, and whatever else you're selling off our property and you'll be locked up for a long time. As I said, you'd better not be here when I come back tonight. This is me giving you a chance, which you do not deserve." He turned to leave.

"Andy, no, wait!" Faye cried. Diana could smell the cheap booze that seemed to ooze from her as she stumbled over to Andy and grabbed his arm, but he shook her off, and she fell back onto the floor, her skirt riding up and the strap of her halter ripping further, slipping down, exposing more of her full breast.

Andy swept his gaze over to Diana. She expected some kind of compassion, but gone was the million-dollar smile, the teasing winks, and the kindness he'd always tossed her way in passing. He fisted his hands as he stared down at her mother, who was still on the floor. "I mean it, Faye. You be out by nightfall, because I'll burn this place to the ground around you if you're not. Should have done it long ago. Told my father to get rid of this house, nothing more than a squatter's shithole."

He yanked open the door and slammed it behind him so hard the windows rattled, and Diana listened as he gunned his engine, hearing the spewing of gravel. Her mother didn't get up but just cried, loud and noisy, on the floor. Louisa started whimpering, and Diana was numbed by what had just happened. This couldn't be real—but it was, far too much so.

Where the hell were they going to go?

She rubbed Louisa's back. "Everything's okay, Louisa. Shh…don't cry. Mama, what are we going to do?" she asked, but her mother only wrapped her arms around her head, crying, stuck in her own misery. Life was so damn unfair. Diana was only thirteen years old, and Andy Friessen had just painted her with the same brush he had her mother.

Five

Diana hadn't been able to get Andy's words out of her head. She shook out a black garbage bag and stuffed in her and Louisa's clothes, all they had, then stared at the bottle of pills her sister took every morning. There were six left, so she tossed them in the garbage bag, too. There were no suitcases or boxes.

The knot in her stomach tightened. Her mother's secrets and whatever she had her hands in now had brought the hammer down on all of them. She folded up the blankets on the bed and then strode down the stairs to the kitchen, glancing once to Louisa, who was playing with the paper bags Diana had found under the sink.

"Can I have that one?" she said and leaned down to Louisa, who held out one of the bags to her. She shook it out, put it on the old counter, and tucked in the plates and cups from the cupboard.

"What are you doing there, girl?" her mother slurred, still drunk, weaving into the kitchen, her hair wet from a shower. She wore a pair of jean shorts and a skintight lowcut t-shirt. At least the stink of sweat and heavy perfume had been washed away, but Diana realized her mother had found another bottle to drown herself in.

"I'm packing. We have to be gone tonight," Diana said. She was still numb, and her stomach knotted not from hunger but from freaking out because she didn't have a clue where they were going to go.

"Well, you just put everything away. We ain't leaving. This is my place. Todd gave this to me. That piece of shit thinks he can just toss me away, well, he's got another thing coming." Faye waved her slender hand, with long red nails, before wandering back into the bathroom, where the hairdryer then whirred.

Louisa ran over to Diana and clung to her leg, rubbing her tired eyes and whining, which was something else her mother couldn't stand. Of course, Louisa was tired from Andy's very angry early-morning outburst, and probably hungry. The tension was so thick in the house that one could have cut it with a knife, and her mother would lose it on Louisa if she didn't stop her whining.

"Louisa, please, honey. Color me a picture," Diana said. She lifted Louisa, carried her into the small living room, and put her down by the old table, where the only coloring book and small box of crayons were, but Louisa wouldn't sit. She threw her crayons and stomped after Diana, screeching in that high-pitched whine, "Go outside, go outside!"

Diana didn't have time for this. She picked Louisa up and carried her with her. Leaning in through the bathroom doorway, she caught a glimpse in the dingy, cracked mirror of a scrawny girl with tangled hair and a tired, pale face holding a skinny, dark-haired imp. Faye was primping like she did every night, and she sprayed her hair, coating it with a layer of hairspray after she had all the curls just right. Her face was coated with heavy makeup, and Diana didn't have a clue what she was doing.

"Mama, Andy said we have to go," she said. Why was her mother not helping, doing something, anything, to find them another place?

Diana watched as Faye reached for the tube of black mascara and applied it to make her already lush lashes even longer. "Andy Friessen is just a hot-headed boy and has overstepped, Diana. He has no right to throw us out. He crossed a line with his temper tantrum. He's just mad about something, and I was the first handy target. Men are like that, you know. They yell, they scream, they lash out, and the next day they forget all about it. So don't you worry none. You put everything back. Now I have to go out. We need some cash, and I know exactly where I'm going to get it."

Whatever that meant, Diana didn't know. Her mother didn't even toss her a glance as she let out a heavy sigh and studied her image in the mirror before striding out of the bathroom, surprisingly steady on her feet even though she was still slurring her words. Diana could hear her rustling in the upstairs closet and knew she was choosing her clothes for the night, something no doubt skintight and revealing.

Diana stood in the open kitchen after putting down Louisa, who was now pulling off her socks. The knot in her stomach had only tightened more. She'd seen the contempt in Andy's eyes and knew he wasn't just blowing off steam. He'd meant everything. He'd condemned her along with Faye, the sins of her mother. *Damn you, Mama! What did you do to Mr. Friessen?*

Diana hated this responsibility, all this worry. This house, this property, was the only home they'd stayed long enough that she could call it home, everything about this place, and she didn't want to leave the few things they had.

Her mother walked out the door, this time without a goodbye, wearing a black dress that barely covered her and heels Diana would never be able to walk in, and Diana listened to her Jeep start up, then turned away from the window and took in the open cupboards in the kitchen where she'd pulled out dishes to pack up. She slowly made her way back in and reached for a box of macaroni beside a jar of peanut butter. She pulled a pot from the cupboard and filled it with water before putting it on the stove to boil, and she hoped that just this one time, maybe her mother was right.

Diana was draining the bathtub, having pulled on her thin blue pajamas after putting Louisa to bed, when she heard the familiar sound of her mother's Jeep. She stepped out into the hall and glanced to the clock on the stove, seeing it was barely ten. She still had the macaroni pot to wash along with the two dirty bowls on the counter.

She heard her mother on the back stairs, then the sound of other vehicles, and she hurried out of the bathroom just as her mother burst through the door. Headlights flickered through the window. A party, seriously? The surrealness of the moment hit her, and she didn't know whether it was the mess in the kitchen or her mother's erratic behavior she feared more in that moment.

Faye slammed the door and bolted it before stepping back, and the knot in Diana's stomach twisted even more as she heard the heavy footsteps outside, then a rattling of the door before it was kicked open, the doorframe splintering. Her mother jumped back and shrieked, and four rough-looking cowboys, one holding a shotgun, strode in, Andy Friessen behind them.

"I told you to be gone, Faye!"

Diana couldn't move. For a moment, she thought her ears were ringing, or was it Louisa whimpering from upstairs? She made herself look to the stairs, not at the cowboys, and then made herself move, running up the stairs to the bedroom she shared with Louisa, who was sitting up in bed, rubbing her eyes. Diana wrapped a blanket around her against the chill in the air, then lifted her in her arms, hearing shouts from downstairs, but she couldn't make out what they were saying.

Her first thought was to hide, but then she heard the creak of the floor, and a strange man in a cowboy hat she'd never seen before was standing in the doorway, gesturing to her, saying, "Come on out of there now. Time to go."

Diana's heart thudded, and she walked barefoot to the bedroom door, where he reached for her arm and pressed his hand to her back. She started down the stairs, the old wood steps creaking. Her mother was already outside, carrying on, crying, shrieking in front of Andy. Two men in jean jackets were standing behind her, and she was on her knees in the dirt, reaching for Andy's arm, begging, "Please, Andy, don't do this! My girls and I have no place to go. How can you throw out a single mom? I've worked out living here with your father. This is our home and my place, fair and square. Your daddy would never allow something like this. Let me call him. Let me talk to Todd. This is just a big misunderstanding…"

What the hell was her mother talking about? Diana was barefoot outside, holding her sister, and she glanced back to the big cowboy behind her, who offered her not even a hint of kindness. For a moment, she hoped Andy would see her and her sister, but he was walking to the side of his fancy pickup and pulling open the passenger door, and she realized it was Todd Friessen who stepped out, holding the door, appearing shaky, pale. Something was wrong. Andy supported his father's arm as if he couldn't stand by himself.

"That's where you're wrong, Faye," Todd said. "I've put up with your shenanigans for a long time, but you went too far last night. If there's one thing everyone in this county is smart enough to know, it's that you don't cross me, ever! You drugged me, you bitch! You're lucky I don't have you thrown in a six-by-three cell for the rest of your life. This is me being generous, because Andy already told you to be out by nightfall. Hear me when I say I'll give you five minutes to grab whatever you want inside, and then I'm having this shack burned to the ground so you can never come back. You leave this county and don't ever set foot back in it."

Diana heard the warning, the anger, but she was numb as she watched the cowboys, who she figured worked for the Friessens, ready to do whatever Todd and Andy told them. The clock was ticking, but her mother just stood there, so Diana raced over to her, still holding Louisa.

"Mama…?" she cried. She shook her mother's arm, and slowly, Faye seemed to pull herself from her stupor and looked down at her. It was dark, but she could see the hurt, the anger, and something else she knew too well.

"This is all *your* fault!" Faye lashed out. "If it weren't for you and that idiot kid, I'd be off living the good life. Guys take one look at you two and go running. I gave up everything because of you."

How much time did they have? Diana didn't have time to feel the slap from her mother as she hurried to the Jeep, pulled open the door, and slid Louisa in the back and buckled her in. "Stay here," was all she said before running barefoot back to the house, past the cowboy who had walked her out. She ran up the stairs to their bedroom and grabbed the garbage bag of clothes, her and Louisa's, before she heard the shout from outside: "Get her out of there and light it up!"

Diana grabbed her shoes at the door just as one of the cowboys started up with a torch. She ran back to the Jeep without looking at Todd, who was leaning against Andy's pickup, and stuffed the bag in back beside her sister, then shoved her bare feet in her shoes.

Andy was standing nose to nose with her mother. His hatred was something she'd never forget. "Faye Claremont, you drive out of here and never show yourself in this county again,"

he said. "I'm done with your games, the whoring, the chasing after my father, the drugs, the booze. Every family in this county will thank me for driving you out of here. Look at you! You're nothing but a two-dollar hooker. Now get the hell off our property, and don't ever show your face here again or you'll be sorry."

Then Andy turned to the cowboys behind him. The one on the old porch was holding a torch, and the front door was wide open. Andy lifted his arm in the air, fisted his hand, and yelled, "Burn it!"

The cowboy walked into the house, there was a whoosh, and then flames flickered as he walked back out. All Diana could do was watch in horror as the only home she'd ever known burned to the ground, taking everything she'd left with it.

She stared at Andy Friessen, a young man she'd sworn to love forever. He'd been her hero, but he'd suddenly become her enemy. And it was in that moment that Diana swore one day, she'd have her justice.

The day was warm and the air conditioning was blasting. Diana had been on the road for hours, and after fifteen years, something was still familiar about the shops of North Lakewood—the hardware store with its blue and white sign, the drug store, which was now a dollar store. Out of the corner of her eye, a cowboy stepped out right in front of her, and she jammed her foot to the brakes so hard that her tires squealed and her heart thudded. She stared in horror as the man slammed his fist on the hood of her SUV. Damn, she'd almost run him down!

His cowboy hat was ratty, and he scowled right at her through the windshield. "Hey, you crazy broad, you trying to kill me? What the hell is wrong with you?"

He was pissed, she got that, but then he stepped around to her window, and she realized he wasn't finished. Evidently, he had something else to say. For a second, she considered ignoring him, but she pressed the button and put her window down.

"I'm sorry. I didn't see you," she said.

He was tall, broad shouldered, with whiskey-colored eyes, and he had no smile for her as he lifted his cowboy hat off to reveal brown hair with natural waves. He shook his head and gestured to the road. "You know what that is right in front of you?" he drawled.

She realized he wasn't going to be nice about this, and she wasn't in the mood to deal with an arrogant cowboy, so she said nothing.

"Not answering? Let me help you. Those are two white lines, which means a crosswalk. The package I was carrying is now broken because I dropped it when you damn near ran me down. What if I'd been a kid? You think about that for a minute."

Now, why the hell had he said something like that? "But you're not," she said. "You're a grown-ass man who should've been watching where you were going. Instead, you stepped right in front of a moving vehicle. I think it's you who should be apologizing to me."

The way he stared at her, she knew he wasn't amused, and she thought he swore under his breath. His hand was resting on her open window, and she let her gaze settle there. "Wow, lady, you really are a piece of work," he said.

Diana made herself look out to the package on the ground, then back to the attractive cowboy with a ton of attitude. Something about him was familiar. She heard a honk behind her. This was exactly what she didn't want to be doing, bringing attention to herself in a place she'd been driven from as just a kid.

"This is ridiculous," she said. "Get away from my vehicle." She waved him off and then rolled up her window, taking in the way he stepped back. She gave her SUV gas and heard a pop as she drove over something, and as she turned the corner, glancing back in the rearview, she caught just a glimpse of the cowboy raising his fist in the air, likely at her. She'd run over whatever was on the ground.

Feeling that fear she'd not felt in so long, she drove down the block, spotted the familiar post office, and parked in front, then glanced up the street, even though it wasn't rational, to see if she'd been followed.

An angry confrontation with a local was exactly what couldn't happen.

"Come on, Diana, get a grip." She let out a shaky breath, resting her hand on the door, considering what she was doing. She was thinking again of that tall, dark-haired young man who'd crushed her and destroyed her life.

She stepped out of her SUV onto a street that was both familiar and different, and she reached for her bulky purse and slipped it over her shoulder before stepping onto the curb and looking right and left, feeling that uncomfortable wave of vulnerability. It had to be this place, so she made herself take a breath and then strode directly up to the door of the old red brick post office. She was dressed in a pink sundress and flat sandals. Her long red hair was tied back in a neat ponytail, and she wore only a hint of makeup.

The post office lady at the counter was in a blue and white uniformed shirt, young, plain, and chatty, the only customer an older woman who left a minute later.

"Can I help you?"

Diana stepped forward, glancing only once to the now closing door. "Yes. I'd like to buy a dozen stamps."

"Certainly." The young woman slid them across the

counter and rang the amount in the register. "I don't recognize you. You from around here?"

Right, Diana was no longer in the city. Small towns were friendly and nosy. "No, not from here. Used to live here when I was young but moved away years ago. A lot about this place hasn't changed, by the looks of it."

The young lady, who she figured was her age, with brown eyes, was now leaning on the counter. "Some hasn't, but a lot has, and not in a good way. Why, I remember, growing up, all we needed were the mom and pop stores, but now it seems everyone goes to the huge commercial shopping mall Mr. Friessen went and built at the edge of town. He gave all the mom and pop stores an option to lease a space out there, and some did move, but the charm of our small town is now, I hate to say it, gone…"

Diana wondered whether her face gave her away. Her stomach knotted when she heard the name. "Mr. Friessen?" she said, doing her best to appear casual, but she wondered if the post office lady had picked up on the squeak in her voice.

"Do you know them? Well, actually, father and son, Todd and Andy Friessen. They own so much around here, or they did. Everyone knows the money comes from Todd's wife. They've bought up so much land and buildings. A family of money but not much else—the marriage, I mean. Come to think of it, I don't think Mrs. Friessen even spends much time here. Heard she has a place in France and down east, too. Old money, you know what I mean, and connected."

She kept her voice low and glanced behind Diana as if making sure no one else was there. "Truth be told, it's quite the scandal. Todd Friessen has a mistress, and everyone knows. He just set her up in the mall with a candy store in a prime spot. It's laughable how in our faces it is. Then there's Andy. Not sure why he goes along with it, although I've heard he's gone a few rounds with his father about the situation, if you know what I mean."

Diana blinked as her stomach knotted again. "So Todd Friessen has another mistress."

The postal girl frowned. "Todd Friessen has always had a mistress. I do believe he's had this one for two years now. Don't know why his wife stays married to him. I've seen her only a few times, but she reminds me of an ice princess, walking around with a pole stuck up her ass. I wonder about men and their mistresses, why they do it. I figure it's all about the money, staying married to a woman you don't love. And that relationship, from what I've heard, is anything but a happy one."

She shrugged, and Diana just stared, feeling the familiar burn of hurt. The woman continued: "Andy, damn, he's got everything going for him. Always wondered why he stands by his father the way he does, because you can see as clear as day how the mention of his father's mistress sets his teeth on edge. For Todd's mistresses, everything's fine as long as he wants you, but just watch out if he decides you're done. That's when Andy gets free rein, and he can run a girl out of town. He's done it, too, and he does it well, from what I've been told. That boy has a meanness when it comes to women—well, women his daddy's been messing around with. Wonder if he knows that's what he's doing, cleaning up for his daddy?"

Diana had to remind herself to breathe.

The postal girl frowned then, really looking at her. "Who'd you say your family was?"

Faye Claremont, her mother, was someone she wanted no one to remember. She lifted her hand and said, "My family's no longer around, been gone for years, but there are some names you don't forget. You know, I remember Andy Friessen and what a big deal he was in the rodeo—or that's what I remember hearing, anyway." She unzipped her wallet and didn't miss the hint of pink on the postal girl's face as she fanned it with her hand.

"Big deal? Oh, let me tell you. That hunk can handle a horse and tame the wildest beast in ways a girl can only dream of. That cowboy could easily win sexiest man of the year, with those broad shoulders or the way he fills out a pair of blue jeans. Tall, dark, and handsome. He really did coin the phrase, let me tell you. He has me stammering like a schoolgirl every time he comes in here, always so damn respectful, polite, friendly. Even remembers my name, and that's a big deal to me. All that man candy is a catch and then some." She made a sound of appreciation, and Diana could only stare at her. She seemed absolutely smitten.

"You've got a crush on him, by the sound of it."

"Who doesn't? I swear, every living, breathing woman in this county and the next has dreamed of settling down with that man since he called off his engagement to the mayor's daughter. It was the longest engagement in history, over ten years. Rumor has it Andy caught her sleeping with his foreman. Threatened to shoot him. Next thing, she up and left town with the guy, and that was the end of that. Just another scandal in a small town."

What was it about hearing his name and all the dirt on the Friessen family that both unsettled Diana and excited her at the same time? She pulled out a ten from her wallet and tucked the stamps she didn't need inside along with the change.

"Thank you for your time and the small-town happenings." She pressed her hand to her stomach, which rumbled. "Oops, sorry. I skipped lunch."

The postal worker gestured to the window. "Merle's is just around the corner, open all day. Restaurant has been here forever, and food's good, too, but you know that if you're from around here."

Diana smiled. The last thing she wanted was to be sitting in a local hangout where someone might have an idea of who she was. She just wasn't ready for that. She lifted her hand in a wave. "Thank you."

"Any time," the postal girl called out.

Diana pulled open the door just as someone was coming in. He was tall, attractive, with a face she'd never forget. After fifteen years, the boy had changed into a man, more solid through the chest and shoulders in his denim shirt, wearing blue jeans that fit too perfectly. From under his black cowboy hat, she could still make out his icy blue eyes, lined with an edge. His large hand was on the door, and she couldn't pull her gaze from his, staring down at her as her heart thudded long and loud in her ears. He narrowed those shrewd eyes at her.

"Diana Claremont?" he said, nothing friendly in his voice. He was blocking the door, and, of course, the post office lady would be hanging on every word. "That red hair is unmistakable, and you're the spitting image of your whore of a mother. When I said leave and don't come back, I meant it. You got that piece of trash, Faye, with you?"

Diana had to remind herself she wasn't that terrified little girl anymore. Andy Friessen was just a bully.

He leaned in. "I will shut down whatever trouble you two are thinking of bringing here, whoring, drugs," he said, and she didn't miss the nasty demand in his voice. Damn, how had she once loved him so deeply?

"Hate to break this to you, but this is not your town," she said. "This is a free country still, and I don't answer to you. So please get out of my way."

Damn, she was proud of herself! But he didn't move. He had a wolflike edge, and the hint of a smile that pulled at the corners of his lips brought a shiver up her spine even though it was so hot out.

"I told you to move out of my way," she said. But he didn't move, so she slipped past him, holding her head high as she hurried down one step and another right to her SUV.

All the while, she knew he was right behind her, but she didn't stop, just pulled open the door, climbed in behind the wheel, shoved her key in the ignition, and started the engine. As she backed out, Andy was on the sidewalk in front of her, watching her, and as she put the car in gear and drove away, she gave one last look in the rearview mirror. Andy Friessen had haunted her dreams with both love and hate, and now he stood with his cell phone to his ear, talking and watching her drive away.

J ed's mood didn't improve much on the forty-minute drive from North Lakewood back to his ranch, hauling his horse trailer after picking up his mare, Scarlett, from the local farrier, who'd informed him she had an abscess on her right front hoof that could, if he didn't keep an eye on it, put her out of commission for the summer. He figured he'd have taken the news better if he weren't still pissed after that redhead had nearly run him down and driven away. Pretty, aggravating, and dangerous.

Jed pulled down his driveway to the forty acres of open land he owned, on which sat a small house that needed a world of work, a barn, and a few older rustic cabins for the dude ranch he was still building. He jammed his foot on the brake when he spotted a silver SUV parked beside his old rusty Ford, then gave his pickup gas as he took in the redhead herself. Her eyes widened, and her mouth opened to say something as he drove past her. He parked his horse trailer behind her

SUV and shut off the engine, and he took his time climbing out of the truck, hiking his jeans up over his slim hips, and taking a deep breath.

"Un-fucking-believable," he muttered. "Small world. You lost?" Even he could hear that he sounded like an asshole. He strode around the back of the rusted single-stall horse trailer and lifted the steel handle that secured the back door. The hinges squealed. He stepped in and murmured to Scarlett, who hung her head and tossed her tail, before he untied her lead rope and led her out, glancing at the redheaded beauty, who had said nothing.

Her long, wavy red hair was pulled back into a ponytail, with strands dangling down over a creamy, pale complexion and sunglasses covering her eyes. She wasn't that tall; the top of her head would probably reach his shoulders. She wore a pink sundress and sandals. Jed let his gaze linger another second as he unlatched the corral gate. Red fumbled her cell phone and swore under her breath before yanking open her driver's door, but instead of hopping in, she tossed the cell phone on the seat and shoved the door closed.

"My phone's dead." She gestured to the SUV, then followed Jed cautiously to the corral beside the small barn. He latched the gate behind him.

"Scarlett, come on, girl," he said as he slid the halter off the dark mare. He looped it and the rope on one of the hooks on the faded barn wall, and then he couldn't help himself: He stared at the fiery, attractive woman but said nothing, letting the awkward silence linger. He dumped a flake of hay on the ground for Scarlett and turned the hose on to fill her water trough. After a few moments, he slid his hand down her side as she drank, and she neighed and flicked her tail. He strode around her to the gate, opened it, and then latched it behind him, very aware of how uncomfortable Red appeared.

"So did you run over anyone else on your way out of town?" he said, then spat on the ground beside him. He didn't really care what she thought.

She pulled her sunglasses off. "Look, I'm sorry. I didn't see you. I was—"

"Lady, you're damn lucky you didn't run over and kill some kid. You were distracted, doing what?" He gestured toward her. "Powdering your nose or whatever the hell you ladies do when you're not paying attention?"

She only pursed her lips, which were full and pink, then glanced to the ground for a second before looking back at him. "I don't really feel like a dressing-down again, if it's all the same. If I could, I'd like to just use your phone. I've apparently found myself lost. I just need to make a call and find out where the cabin I've rented is. It's at a dude ranch, but the directions I have…" She gestured again, looking around, and frowned.

"What are you looking for?" He didn't move, and he realized his response had been sharper than he meant.

The redhead kept her cool and unfolded the piece of paper clutched in her hand. "A place called Echo Springs. The directions I have here are to head down the highway—"

Jed shut his eyes, feeling that kick from the universe again. He lifted his worn cowboy hat and wiped the sweat from his forehead. "Seriously?" was all he said. He stared at the confusion in those bright blue eyes, picturing the calendar in the house with a name written on it, the only guest at his ranch that week. He put his hat back on and gestured to her. "Small world. Hate to tell you this, but you're not lost. So you're Diana Fulton."

Her eyes widened, and her face paled, and he thought she swore under her breath. Then she gestured to his house, his barn, and said, "You can't be serious. This doesn't look anything like the photos on the internet. Where're the gorgeous shaded cabins, the green grass and rolling hills, or how about just some patio furniture? This is nothing more than a shithole dustbowl…"

"What the hell, lady? This ain't some five-star resort. This is a ranch. Not sure what you thought you were booking, but a dude ranch is about you and a horse, not a day at the spa." He wondered, though, whether he should ask where she saw the details online about his ranch. The booking form was direct and to the point, mentioning the cabin and the ranch experience. Then there were pack trips and overnight camping in the mountains, but the only group he'd booked for that was a family of four in two weeks. The lady standing there now appeared completely out of her element.

She was looking around again, and he wondered if she'd demand her money back, so he pulled his arms over his chest and said, "The grass is green in the spring, but this time of year is hot and dry. You want some upscale, fancy place, you're in the wrong part of the country. No idea where you'd get a harebrained idea like that. You booked online for a cabin over there, and to be clear, there are no refunds."

The fact was that he'd already spent the money on supplies to repair the leaky roof before the rain started. He took in his place, seeing all the repairs he still needed to do. However, it was still his paradise.

She said nothing, then, "I need a second."

What was he supposed to do, just stand there while she decided to drive away or argue with him? He figured the latter, by the looks of her. "Well, that was five. You figured it out yet? Because I have work to do."

She let her gaze linger, a spark in her blue eyes. He figured he was already on her bad side. "Can I see the cabin?"

He glanced at her SUV, then walked over to the horse trailer, closed up the back, and gestured ahead. "Well, come on," he said. "Don't have all day."

He started walking past her toward his small bungalow and the three cabins about a hundred yards, give or take, from the house. They sat just behind a crop of pine trees, the only ones on the property, which gave him and his guests privacy. He knew his strides were long, and he didn't slow his pace until he stopped in front of the first cabin and waited for her, watching as she stepped around a pile of manure he hadn't picked up yet.

"Here's where you're bunking," he said. "Bunk against the wall. Outhouse is around back, outdoor shower beside it." The step to the cabin was just a crate, and he stepped up on it and opened the door. At least he'd taken a broom to it. He gestured inside, bumping the wooden bunk.

She was standing right beside him, and he wondered why she hadn't climbed in her SUV and driven out of there. "No kitchen?" she said, lifting her chin. She was standing so close to him that he had to rest his arm on the top bunk.

He made a face. "Lady, these cabins aren't for long stays. Everyone who comes is planning on being on a horse the next day and spending nights in a tent, with dinner cooked over a fire. This is a camp for cowboys. You get a bunk and a cabin the night before we head out. So no, as you can see, there's no kitchen. You can use the fridge in my house if needed. I make coffee in the morning, and you can make whatever you want. Just clean up after yourself."

She said nothing, still standing there, staring at the wooden bunk, the foam mattress.

"Look, I'm going to help you out here, because this is really painful," Jed said. "As you can see, you won't fit here. This isn't a place of comfort or lounging around. I can see you made a mistake, figuring this was something it wasn't, so let's save each other from trying to figure out something polite to say. There're a few motels and a hotel in town with everything there or close by—"

"No," she said. "I paid for it, I'll take it. As you said, no refunds." She had cut him off, and for a second, he wanted to laugh. He had to wonder if it was just her stubborn pride.

"Suit yourself," he said, stepping off the crate onto the hard packed dirt.

"Wait. You haven't told me your name," Diana called out to him.

He turned back, lifting the brim of his hat, taking in the pretty thing. "Jed Friessen," he said. "Just call me Jed. Again, if you decide this isn't for you, pick a direction, ten miles, give or take. Either way, you'll find something more to your liking."

She didn't say anything, and he wasn't sure what to make of her expression.

"If you need anything," he continued, "I have some cleanup to do in the barn." He gestured to it. She only nodded, and this time, when Jed started walking, Diana Fulton said nothing at all.

Diana stared at the plywood walls of the smallest cottage she'd ever seen, with its wooden bunk and old foam mattress. She listened to the footsteps of a tall, rugged, handsome cowboy walking away, reeling because this had to be a fucking joke. Friessen? He'd said his name was Jed Friessen.

She wasn't sure if she should cry or laugh, either, over this dump of a cabin she'd booked. How had she missed the fact that "rustic" meant barely one step up from a tent? The one small window was missing a screen, and there was no dresser, just a rickety side table beside the wooden platform and a couple hooks on the wall. She pictured the outhouse out back and strode over to the open door in time to watch that handsome cowboy walk away. She hoped he wasn't related to Andy, but, knowing her luck, she'd just driven into the vipers' nest.

She took in the crate and stepped down onto the dirt. Her painted pink toenails would be dirty in no time, but Diana had learned long ago to deal with whatever was tossed her way. She understood too well the feeling of loss, of having nothing. The cowboy walked into the oldest barn she'd ever seen, and she took in the small house he lived in. So much about the place seemed run down and under construction, judging by the pile of wood covered with a tarp. Jed walked back out of the barn with a wheelbarrow and pitchfork toward a pile of manure and dumped it.

"This is going to sound silly, but I didn't bring any bedding or towels," she called out.

He said nothing as he finished cleaning up the manure, one scoop and another. Damn, his silence was unnerving. She tried to see the resemblance, if any, to Andy. Finally, he looked over to her, and it was painful how he said nothing.

"But I can purchase some supplies tomorrow when I get into town," she said. "Evidently, I assumed everything would be supplied, like in a hotel or even a motel."

Why the hell was she so nervous? She took in those whiskey-brown eyes and wavy hair under the rattiest cowboy hat she'd ever seen. His face had whiskers, likely from a day or two without shaving. Something about him and this place made it seem impossible for him to be related to Andy. Maybe Friessen was a common name out there, like Smith or Johnson?

"You didn't bring bedding?"

She felt her face heat and made herself stand her ground. "I'm sorry, I didn't. I just brought my clothes, essentials. I assumed everything would be here. I didn't see any plugin for my laptop, either. You have electricity, internet access?"

Again, the silence was painful. This man, she figured, had coined the phrase "strong, silent type."

"Nope, no electricity. Again, there are no comforts of home here, just a bunk to sleep. Everyone who books a stay is on a horse the next day, headed to one of the camps. You get the ground and a sleeping bag and only what can be packed easily on horseback. I have internet inside for my computer, but no wireless, and cell service out here is spotty." He let his gaze linger, then rested the rake by the wheelbarrow and shook his head before he started walking to the small bungalow, up the rickety steps and inside.

She was wondering whether that was it, he was done listening to her, when she spotted him walking out again with a sleeping bag under his arm and what looked like a towel.

"Hope you can make do with these," was all he said, and her heart did a little flip as he handed them to her, a dark blue sleeping bag, rolled up tight, and a worn green towel.

"Thank you. I can." She took in the way he watched her, no smile, nothing. Then he gave a nod and walked back over to the wheelbarrow, but not before she said, "I don't think I apologized for nearly running you down."

Jed pulled his hat off and ran his large hands through his thick, wavy brown hair. "Was that an apology? Needs some work, if it was."

So graciousness was not part of this cowboy's vocabulary. She found herself fisting the sleeping bag, reminding herself she'd been the one to drive away. "I'm sorry, but again, you did just step out in front of me, crosswalk or not. Did no one ever teach you to look both ways before you cross and make sure the driver sees you before you step out?"

A flicker of something pulled at the corners of his lips—a smile, amusement? Maybe. "Touché," he said. "How about we just leave it there?"

Some of the tension that had pulled across Diana's shoulders eased, and she breathed in the warm air, the dryness, the heat, and let her gaze linger on the horse in the corral. "I've never ridden a horse. Always wanted to learn. If I pay you, will you teach me?"

He didn't answer for the longest time, just watched her. She wondered for a moment whether he'd say no. Then his gaze dropped to her sandals. "Hope you packed something better than those and that dress. I can teach you, but you won't be getting anywhere near my horse with open-toed sandals."

The breeze rustled the thin cotton of her sundress. "I wore this for comfort while I was traveling because it's so hot. I have jeans and a pair of hiking boots. Anything else I need I'll pick up in town when I go."

He nodded without pulling his gaze. Damn, he was a hard man to read. "Well, then, get settled and changed. Meet me back here in an hour and I'll introduce you to your ride. But come prepared. You want to learn about horses and how to ride one, you're going to get dirty." Then he gave her a nod, lifted the handle of the wheelbarrow, and started walking back to the barn, and all she could do was stare at the sexy cowboy walking away. There was nothing pretty about him. No, everything about him left her with the feeling that he wasn't one to play around with a woman or toss her aside just because he could.

"Is this the horse you'll teach me to ride?" Diana said. Her red hair was so vibrant and bright, and her blue eyes reminded him of the prettiest blue skies. She was slender and curvy, wearing a pair of faded blue jeans and a plain red t-shirt. She rested her hands on the top bar of the corral while Jed finished picking up the manure, and Scarlett walked over, swishing her tail.

He let his gaze linger on her boots, which appeared worn. Her hair was brushed back into a ponytail, and her face, he realized, wasn't painted up, like so many of the women he'd come across.

"Tell me what you know about horses," he said. "Your experience, how much riding you've done." He moved the wheelbarrow to another pile of manure and scooped.

"I love horses, but I've never ridden," she said. "Not once. Never had the opportunity, and I never allowed myself to have that dream. I've always admired them from afar. There's something about them, you know.

They know things, smell things before we do. It's as if they speak another language, and I've wanted to understand them, how they think, why they get spooked or jumpy."

She stayed outside the corral while he finished dumping the manure in the wheelbarrow, then lifted the rake over the rail and leaned it against the barn wall. Diana let her gaze linger on Scarlett. God damn, she was beautiful.

"Well, at least you're smart enough to know that much about a horse, though you've never ridden," he said, knowing it had come out sharply. "Most people figure they can just jump in the saddle, kick the horse a couple times, yank and pull the reins, and they're in control. That stupidity is a good way to get yourself thrown and killed." He wheeled the wheelbarrow through the gate and latched it behind him, then headed to the manure pile on the other side of the barn, where he dumped the wheelbarrow out. He turned to see her still lingering by the corral, and he started back to her.

"If you want to learn about horses, to ride, this is what you'll be doing every morning," he said. "You'll need to help out. It's my rule on this ranch, which comes with the lessons. I'll take you out on the trail when you're comfortable, but when you're learning about horses, you're going to do everything. You can't be worrying about a broken fingernail or whether your delicate skin is burning or your butt is sore. Your horse is always looked after and tended to first. If you look after your horse, she'll look after you. Understand? You're starting with the basics so I can see what you can do."

He stopped in front of her, and she stiffened, a question in her eyes. She looked into the distance. What was she thinking?

"Well, come on." He started walking to the barn and inside, where the concrete needed a good sweep. He didn't wait for her to catch up. "Here's the tack room, where I keep the saddles, blankets, halters, brushes, everything you need to care for your horse. Grab a curry comb, brush, and hoof pick, and we'll start with those."

Jed pointed to the tack box on the floor, hoping she'd figure it out. She strode past him, squatted down to the box, and grabbed one of each. He was already walking again, and she hurried to catch up to his long strides. He was at the corral gate, Scarlett on the other side, and he opened it.

"First and foremost, with gates on a farm, you always double-check and make sure they're latched. Never leave a gate open or unlocked for a second, thinking you'll be right back. That's how animals get out and accidents happen. The horses could get hurt or killed."

Diana clutched the brush, pick, and comb to her as she walked into the corral and Jed closed the gate behind her. Scarlett nickered when he walked toward her.

"This is Scarlett," he said. "She's an Appaloosa Quarter Horse, eight years old, the sweetest thing. You'll be riding her, and you'll look after her—and she'll look after you."

"What's she like?" Diana said as she lifted one hand, trembling a bit, and cautiously touched Scarlett's side. She was terrified but stronger than he'd expected.

"If you're nervous, shake it off before you come in here, because she'll pick up on it and test you. It's hard to break that once she's got you pegged. She's reading your body language, how you walk, how you approach her, your hesitation, what you're thinking. Being scared or unsure tells her only one thing—she can't trust you. And you don't ever want to be on a horse that doesn't trust you."

Diana flicked her gaze to him, startled and thinking way too much.

"Give her a good brushing," he said.

She lifted the brush and stepped closer to Scarlett, hesitant still. That was when the mare moved, nearly knocking her over. Jed stepped in and smacked Scarlett's hind end, pushing her away.

"Hey, move over. Behave yourself," he said. He reached down and grabbed Diana's hand with his large, rough one, then shoved a ragged plastic curry comb in it and placed it on Scarlett's side. "Move in closer. Here, press here, and rub in circles like this. Show her you mean it, like you know what you're doing. *Think* about what you're doing *before* you do it. If you hesitate, she'll know it before you do. Understand that she's testing you now. Score one for Scarlett—she pushed you over. Next time, she'll walk on you.

"Now you have to undo what you've just reinforced. Sometimes it's ten times harder to undo a mistake than it is to get things right the first time. That's your first lesson. When you don't know what to do, or you're scared as hell, she'll walk all over you, and you'll lose her trust. Once she's in charge, it's damn hard to reverse the roles. So when you come in here with her, have a plan. Your hand is always touching her side, like this, so she knows where you are. You comb her, brush her.

"Always have your hand on her when you walk

behind her, and walk close behind. You don't want to give her room to kick you. If she kicks you, she'll break your leg. And startled horses will kick. So I'll repeat it again: Make sure she knows where you are at all times. After you've got her brushed down, you'll hoof pick. I'll walk you through all of this today. Then we'll start some groundwork so you and Scarlett can get to know each other."

He made himself move away and let go of her hand. He hadn't expected his reaction to her, and the way she glanced up at him, he felt the energy being kicked up between them. He cleared his throat as he stepped back again and gestured toward Scarlett.

"Finish brushing her. Focus on her," he said. There was something about her personality, a calmness and something else he couldn't put his finger on. "So what do you do, Diana?"

She hesitated as she brushed and glanced over to him, and he wasn't sure what he was seeing in those sky-blue eyes. Damn, she was gorgeous. "I presume you mean for a living…"

He meant a lot of things. "Well, for starters, you're in the middle of nowhere, renting a piece-of-shit cabin and taking lessons from me to learn to ride a horse. You're not from here, so where are you from, and why are you here? What do you do for a job?"

She kept brushing and glanced again over to him. "I'm a lawyer—well, junior. Just passed the bar and still deciding on where to set up a practice for myself. Option two is to apply for a junior position in a big law firm and be shoved into a corner cubby, doing wills, paperwork, subpoenas, or filing motions all day, every day, working an eighty-hour week and not having a life.

You know, the boring grunt work. There's no way in hell that's going to happen, so I'm sticking with option one and setting up my own practice to do what I want. And you don't give yourself enough credit, Mr. Friessen…"

"Jed," he said. "My name is Jed. The only people who call me Mister are bill collectors, tax agents, and bankers before they turn me out of their office, demand money, or take more of what isn't theirs. And I'm pretty sure you're not one of them, are you, Diana?"

A smile pulled at the corners of her lips, and there was a sparkle of amusement or something in those amazing blue eyes. It lit up her whole face as she kept brushing and gave her head a shake. "Well, I stand corrected, Jed. But this place… Although the cabin is not much, or less than that, it's a roof over my head. More of a rustic holiday than I planned, but I've lived with less."

He wasn't sure what to make of her last comment. "You didn't say where you're from. What made you come out here to this?"

She was really digging in with her brushing, focused. "Portland, originally, and I went to law school in Spokane, but I'm considering setting up shop out here."

His heart thudded. Something about the thought of her sticking around had him feeling things he hadn't in a long time. "Well, I hope you do."

There it was again, the smile, the way she let her gaze linger. Her hand rested on Scarlett's side as she nickered, tossing her head as if sensing Diana's discomfort, and his. This time, when Scarlett tried to bump Diana and step on her foot, she smacked her hind end just like Jed had and said, "No, move over."

Damn, he hadn't expected that.

Diana sat in her parked SUV in town. She had taken a cold shower when the sun rose and grabbed a quick coffee from Jed's kitchen, then, as he'd told her the night before, helped herself to some cereal.

There was something about the edgy cowboy that she couldn't get out of her mind as she climbed out of her car, holding a handful of flyers with her name and cell phone number, advertising and outlining the legal services she offered. Diana knew her fee was reasonable, and her first stop would be the post office, with its bulletin board in back. She tacked up the white paper, waved to the postal worker, whom she recognized from the day before, and made her way out.

The empty glass commercial storefronts in town all had for-rent signs, but renting one now wasn't in her budget, and she knew that because Todd and Andy had influence in this town, nothing would be available for her. How was it that a mother she hadn't seen in years continued to leave an unwelcome legacy for her?

She knew she needed to let it go, but that was only one of the reasons she was back in North Lakewood now. She tacked up flyers on lampposts and at bus stops, the gas station, and the library. For good measure, she used the free Wi-Fi at the library and posted an ad on the community website, too. Satisfied she had done all she could, and after her stomach rumbled again, she knew she needed to pick up some food, groceries, and drive back to Jed's ranch, where she felt unbelievably welcome.

She pushed open the door to the family-owned grocery store, which appeared the same as it had when she was a kid, and reached for a cart, taking in the same dingy green tiles on the floor. The unease that had disappeared after a day at Jed's was now back. Her memories of a place that had hurt her so badly had her looking over her shoulder.

"You're being ridiculous," she told herself in a low voice as she headed through the produce section and glanced up to the large oval security mirror mounted close to the ceiling. She wore sandals and a blue and white sundress with cap sleeves, conservative. For a second, she froze, but she forced herself to keep moving. She stopped at the apples and bagged half a dozen, then some lettuce and tomatoes.

She was thinking of a mild cheddar cheese when she spotted Mr. Harris standing at the back of the store, watching her. The way his brows narrowed as he focused on her, she realized he recognized her, so she made herself look away. She grabbed a carton of whole milk and a block of marble cheese instead of looking for anything else, then hurried down the aisle and found mayo and pickles. She went to the deli and bakery for some sandwich meat and bread, then picked up some chicken for dinner and a few other condiments, all the while unable to shake the feeling of unease as she fought the urge to look over her shoulder.

She made her way up to the only cashier, a young, overweight girl who greeted Diana with a bubbly smile.

"Did you find everything?" She had a slight twang, and Diana wondered if she was new to the area.

"I did, thank you," Diana said as she quickly unloaded her groceries. Just then, the cashier's phone rang, and when the girl answered, Diana didn't miss the way her brown eyes lingered a little too long on her. Something about it was too familiar, and it brought that giant ache.

"Yes, sir, Mr. Harris. I understand." The cashier was no longer smiling. "I'm sorry, miss, but I'm not allowed to serve you. Mr. Harris, the store owner, said to tell you you're not welcome here."

Shock was all Diana could feel as she stared at the groceries she needed. She had money to pay for them, but the cashier was already moving them aside. "Mr. Harris told you what, exactly?" she said, then glanced behind her, feeling the heat of embarrassment. She wondered whether he was watching her now through the security camera.

"Please, I need this job," the cashier said. "Just go. I'm not sure what the problem is, but I don't want to be stuck in the middle. This is private property and a private business, and he has the right to refuse service to anyone."

Diana knew she was right, but this wasn't okay. "Where is he?" was all she said.

The cashier hesitated only a second, then pointed. "In back, in his office."

Diana took in the exit and knew she should just walk out, but she was done with being bullied, so she lifted her purse over her shoulder and strode down the bulk food aisle to the back double doors, praying she'd figure out what to say by the time she reached them. They opened right before she got there, and out walked Mr. Harris, a big man who looked down on her with nothing friendly.

"You were told to leave this store, Faye Claremont."

"I'm not Faye," she said. "That was my mother. I'm Diana Fulton."

He stepped back, and his face flushed with a hint of red, anger or embarrassment. "Don't matter much," he said. "Mother, daughter. Faye turned this town upside down. She was a stain on this place, a bad apple, and so were her kids. The Friessens sending you packing was the best thing for everyone here. Now get out before I call the sheriff and have you arrested for trespassing."

The only problem with being a lawyer was that she understood how right he was. He could ban her forever from walking through the doors.

"Fine, I'll go," she said. "But shame on you. I'm not Faye Claremont. Maybe, if there's any justice, one day someone will judge you for something your father did." Then she turned away, realizing she was shaking.

"Don't set one foot back in here," he said. "You can't fool me, girlie! You're the same trash as your mama. You get out and don't come back…"

Diana's face was burning, and the cashier's big eyes stared at her in horror. She reached into her purse and pulled out a business card, then walked right up to the cashier and held it out to her. "I'm a lawyer. If you're ever in need of legal help, call me. That's my cell number."

The young cashier frowned but took the card, and Diana kept walking right out of the store and over to her SUV. She pulled the door open and stared back at the small-town grocery store, knowing her mother's legacy was still alive and well in North Lakewood.

But her carefully laid-out plan wasn't to get justice for herself. It was for her little sister, who'd hurt no one.

"Louisa, I swear I'll make them pay," she said. It was a promise she'd made long ago, and even though she'd waited this long, something about being back there now in the wolfs' den made her realize this wasn't going to be as easy as she thought.

She backed out and drove back to Jed's ranch, knowing it was only a matter of time before everyone who knew her mother would be asking what Faye Claremont's daughter was doing back in North Lakewood.

She parked beside Jed's older brown pickup and spotted him walking out of the barn.

"Was expecting you half an hour ago," he called out.

Right, lessons with Scarlett. But she still needed groceries. "Sorry," she said. "I was tacking up flyers and went to pick up some groceries as well." She walked over to the old barn, where Jed was holding a set of reins. She stopped in front of him, and he glanced over to her SUV and back to her.

"You want to take the groceries in and get changed?" he said. "I'll meet you in the barn. That dress is pretty, but not around horses. I'll teach you to saddle up today and get you on her."

Damn, he really was nice, but he had no idea who she was. She wondered if she'd winced.

"Would you be okay if we postponed the lessons until this evening?" she said. "I actually need to make a run to Arlington for groceries. I appreciate the cereal this morning, but…"

He frowned and shook his head. "I thought you said you were getting groceries in town. What, do they not carry something to your liking?" She didn't miss the edge in his voice. Boy, she'd really given him the wrong impression.

"No, nothing like that," she said. "I just ran into some issues."

His brown eyes reminded her of deep, dark whiskey, and the way he watched her, she would've sworn he could see right into her soul. He frowned again. "What kind of issues? Seems pretty simple: You drive to the store, grab a few things, pay for them, and leave. I realize the grocery store in town is small, but I've never had trouble finding what I needed."

Diana reminded herself that her reality wasn't his. She could just make out a brown chestnut in the stall inside the barn, and she wondered how many horses Jed had. "Normally, yes. This isn't about me not finding what I needed. I had everything and was trying to pay for it, but…" She stopped talking because the words just wouldn't come.

"You don't have enough money?"

She flicked her gaze up to him rather sharply. "I have money, my money. In fact, I'm damn good at saving and paying for everything. Sometimes it's got nothing to do with that and everything to do with small-minded people. The fact is that Mr. Harris, who owns the store, refused to sell anything to me and ordered me to leave, and if I didn't, he was going to call the sheriff and have me arrested. So now, because of that pompous ass, I have to drive to Arlington for groceries."

She hadn't meant for it to come out so sharply. Jed had gone still, not pulling his gaze, in which she saw shock and surprise.

He shook his head. "And why would old Jason Harris do that?"

Diana didn't cower. She wouldn't do that with anyone, not even with the intensity staring back at her, the edge simmering in Jed's brown eyes as he waited for her to come clean. "Because of who my mother was."

Diana filled the old bathtub that served as a water trough for Scarlett. She'd changed into faded blue jeans, a dark blue t-shirt, and her hiking boots. Her gaze lingered again on the driveway Jed had driven his pickup down after up and leaving without a word. It seemed like moments ago but had likely been more than an hour.

She swore she'd never forget his voice, the way he'd said, rather sharply, "Stay here," before jumping in his truck and sending gravel and dust spewing as he left. She recognized the anger and frustration of a man close to losing it, and she'd had a moment of unease, wondering where he was going, what he was doing. She knew he was likely now standing face to face with Mr. Harris, a man, just like many in this town, who'd had no use for her mother or for her.

It may have happened fifteen years earlier, but Diana would never forget that unwanted feeling or the disdain that had been tossed her way by the people of North

Lakewood all because she'd been Faye Claremont's daughter.

Her hand was shaking as she turned off the water, and she shut her eyes for a second before turning to the horse. She wondered whether she'd ever have a chance to ride her. She already knew Jed would be told every unflattering thing. The gossips would be in full swing, and she didn't know anyone who had the courage to stand against it and maybe just think for themselves. Maybe that was what hurt more than anything. She didn't want Jed to be one more who looked at her unkindly. What was it about having her character torn apart, and people just blindly believing whatever they were told, that hurt so much?

Gravel crunched on the long driveway, and Diana glanced up from where she leaned against the barn. Her bags were packed, as the next words out of Jed's mouth were likely going to be cold and cruel. Her heart thudded as Jed, behind the wheel of his pickup, pulled in, dust trailing. She suddenly had trouble swallowing. Her heart thudded, and she couldn't get the damn shaking inside her to stop. She forced herself to push away from the barn and made herself walk over to the gate, unlatch it, and step out.

She had just latched it behind her when Jed climbed out of his truck and slammed the door. Another pickup was coming down the driveway, dark blue and brand-new with tinted windows, and it pulled in beside Jed's truck. When the driver climbed out, she shut her eyes, knowing this was worse than she'd imagined.

"What the hell are you doing here?" Jed said to him, his tone not unfriendly.

Andy was in blue jeans and a light blue dress shirt,

and he walked right over to Jed, shook his hand, and clapped his shoulder. She thought she heard laughter, and in that second, everything fell into place. There was closeness between them. She didn't have a clue what to do, and she realized both men were looking her way.

She had to remind herself she wasn't that terrified little girl anymore. She made herself take a step. She had fisted her hands, and she relaxed them as she said, "Well, hello, Andy."

Jed said nothing, staring first at Andy and then over to Diana. "You two know each other?" he finally said. "What brings you out here, cuz?"

Friessen. Of course they were related. She stared in horror at the confusion that appeared on Jed's face and the hardness on Andy's. Side by side, she could see it. The family resemblance was uncanny. Damn, she'd hoped she wouldn't be right.

"You have a visitor out here, I see," Andy said. "Someone who shouldn't be here."

Jed didn't pull his gaze from Andy, and the tension ramped up. Why wasn't Jed saying anything?

"What are you doing here, Diana?" Andy said. "I told you to get out of town and never come back."

"You can't tell me what to do, Andy," she said. "You have no say in my life. If I want to move back here, that's my right."

Diana had known on some level there would be a confrontation with Andy, but she hadn't expected this, and not so soon. She pulled her arms over her chest, feeling that uncomfortable vulnerability. The way Andy stared at her, she realized he still terrified her. *He has no power over me,* she tried to remind herself.

"No, it's not." Andy didn't look away. "You got that whore of a mother with you? Where is she?"

She'd never forget the anger in his voice from that night so long ago. It was the same now. She had to remind herself to stay calm. "I have no idea where Faye is, not that I'd tell you, anyway."

Jed went still, not pulling his gaze from Andy, and she feared what he must think of her.

"I see you want to play games with me," Andy said. "You were told to leave and never come back."

Diana was shaking inside, but she made herself look Andy square in the eye. "You told my mother that. I was just a kid. And there's no way in hell you have any say in where I go or what I do. You can't make me leave."

"Well, that's where you're wrong," Andy said. "Jed, throw her out."

Diana realized maybe she shouldn't have left her packed bag sitting in the cabin. That old, familiar panic had stung the back of her throat as Andy tossed out the order, and she watched Jed pull his arms across his chest, really settling into his stance. He didn't look her way.

"What the fuck is wrong with you, Andy?" he said. "You don't order me to do anything on my property, not ever. You two seem to have a history, and I'm not liking what I'm hearing so far."

Jed still hadn't pulled his gaze from Andy, and Diana didn't know what to do. She stared at a man who wasn't falling into line with Andy's orders. So much about Jed confused her.

"Jed, listen to me," Andy said. "You don't want this piece of trash here. She's a Claremont looking for a meal ticket. Her and that mother of hers will be bringing drugs in here, selling them, whoring, conniving…" Andy gestured rather sharply to her.

Jed glanced her way for only a second, but it was a second in which she saw the confusion and the open question in his eyes.

"Look, Jed, she was trained by the best. She'll destroy you. She doesn't care who she hurts. She'll rob you blind." Andy dragged his gaze back to Diana, letting it linger on her breasts in a way that had her wanting to slap him. Damn, why would he do this to her? She'd never done anything to him. It had been her mother, and she still didn't know every horrible thing Faye had done.

Diana pulled her arms over her breasts, trying to hide herself. "Please stop, Andy," she said. "I'm not my mother. I never did any of that. I do not do drugs or drink. I was just a kid, and you took everything from me. And for the record, my name isn't Claremont anymore. It's Diana Fulton."

Why was Jed not saying anything? He glanced to her again, confusion lingering in those whiskey-brown eyes.

"Mrs. Fulton, is it?" Andy said. "What did you do, marry some guy and take him for everything he had, and now you've set your sights on my cousin?"

She felt the slap even though he hadn't touched her. For a moment, she couldn't get her tongue to move. Her eyes stung with tears, and she was thinking back to a night so long ago that had shaped her into who she was today. "I've never been married," she said. "I was adopted by a very kind, loving older couple who gave me their name. They died in a car accident, a five-car pile-up on their way to visit me in my first year of law school."

She couldn't get anything else out, blinking back the tears, pulling her hand over her eyes, remembering the hours she had waited and they never came. The way Andy watched her now was with something she didn't recognize—shame, shock, something. She could feel Jed watching her intently, too, and the remembered rawness of losing everything in one night was an unwelcome companion.

"Sorry. I didn't know. I shouldn't have said that," Andy said. He gestured to her, and there was something awkward there.

"No, you didn't know," she said. "But then, concern for others' feelings has never been the trait of a Friessen."

There was an edge to Andy again, and even she felt the bite of her words. Damn, she was making a mess of this, but she wanted him to feel the hurt, that pain, even just a little of what she had.

"That coming from the daughter of Faye Claremont is a little like the pot calling the kettle black," he said. "Giving a shit about anyone other than herself was not what your mother did."

Diana squeezed her fists, feeling the anger driving her as she took another step closer. "I never hurt anyone, ever. Me and Louisa just got caught in the midst of a battle we never signed on for. We didn't deserve to be treated like dirt or to be tarred and feathered, which is what you did. That was your fight with Faye, not us. She may have done something to your father, but you seem to forget Louisa and I paid the ultimate price for it. We were just two terrified little kids who wanted someone to give a damn about us, and suddenly we were collateral."

Diana took another step, slapped both her hands to

Andy's chest, and shoved, but he didn't budge. Jed was right there, his hand on her arm, stepping between them.

"Diana, enough," he said. "I need you both to stop before this goes sideways. And for the record, Diana, I'm a Friessen, and I've never taken advantage of anyone or knowingly hurt someone. So both of you need to knock it off, because I'm not liking everything I've heard so far."

Diana pulled away from Jed, taking a step back. "I was only thirteen, Andy. You had no right to do what you did. And every action has consequences. I lost everything that night, my mother, my home, everything I owned. And Louisa. She died. You burned our house down, giving me only a minute to grab what I could…" Her voice was strangely distant.

Andy appeared confused, then gave his head a shake, and there it was, the arrogance in his expression that had her wanting to slap it off his face. "That's quite the story, Diana. God damn, for a minute, I almost believed you. But you know what? That reminds me of Faye, because no one was better at spinning a hard-luck, been-done-wrong story than she was. I can't help thinking, like mother, like daughter. She taught you well, but it won't work on me."

That had her taking a step. She struck his face, but he was fast, grabbing her wrist as she tried to withdraw, holding tight.

"Andy, I'm warning you, let her go." Jed was right there, his hand on Andy.

Andy let go of her wrist, holding his hand up, taking a step back. She felt the burn of where he'd touched her, and he touched his face where she'd slapped him, where she'd left the imprint of her hand.

"And you step back, too," Jed said. The way he was looking at her, she could feel his anger. She heard the warning, and she fisted her hand again and pulled her arms over her chest. This confrontation was going nowhere.

"Why'd you come back here, Diana?" Andy said. "What's this really about, money, revenge, destroying me and my father, getting to us through my cousin? And where's Faye? You still haven't answered me. Hiding, sneaking around, planning…"

Diana couldn't look at Jed. She felt ashamed that Andy could so easily toss out another story about her that wasn't true. "I didn't know Jed was your cousin," she said, and she let her gaze linger on him. "All I can say is it seems the universe has an odd sense of humor. I have no idea where my mother is. I haven't seen her since the night you burned us out. She left me and my sister in her Jeep, parked outside a bar in Portland late at night. She said she needed cash. You're right that she did everything, drugs, booze, men. She tried to sell drugs to the wrong man, an undercover cop, and she was arrested. The cops took me and my sister.

"You know Louisa took pills every day for seizures? I couldn't find the bottle I'd packed in the garbage bag where I'd tossed a few of our things. She had a seizure at the stationhouse while we waited for a social worker, probably from the stress of everything. They took her to the hospital but wouldn't let me go with her. I was placed in foster care, an emergency place, as they called it. My sister died alone. I wasn't even allowed to see her. Does my mother even know?" Diana shrugged. "I have no idea. All I know is she was given ten years in prison for child endangerment and selling drugs, and my sister was buried in a state grave with only a marker. Did I come back here for a reason? Damn right I did. What you and your father did all those years ago was wrong, not only illegal but wrong. So I worked my way through law school, learned what my rights really are. I saw how too many take the rights of those who can't fight back. I understand how the law really works, how it's manipulated. I'm no longer that terrified little kid who can be bullied by you and your father."

Andy angled his head, and those icy blue eyes held a warning. She knew not to toy with him. "That sounds like you're threatening me, Diana," he said. "Word of advice? Don't pick a fight with me, because I guarantee you'll get hurt. You come after me or my father and I'll fucking bury you. Here's your friendly warning: Pack your bags, go back to where you came from, and get on with your life, because it's not here. The doors in this town will always be closed to a Claremont. Conniving, scheming… From what I'm hearing, it sounds as if you're picking up where your mother left off. You say you haven't heard from her, so you better hope for your sake that she doesn't come sniffing back around."

Andy let his gaze linger on her again, dragging it over her. What the hell was he thinking? He shook his head and said, "You know, your story is almost believable, but the problem is you're the spitting image of your mother, and that isn't a good thing for you."

Even though Andy hadn't touched her, the slap of his words hurt more than anything. She'd been cast under Faye's shadow.

She felt Jed's hand on her arm, and he was standing

right in front of her, gesturing to his pickup. He said, "Diana, your groceries are in the truck. Go grab them and take them into the house. Put them away before the ice cream melts."

Diana wasn't ready to walk away. She still had a few more things to say to Andy. But Jed had maneuvered her away from him, and the fact was that he wasn't asking her to leave. He had picked up her groceries. Why?

She only nodded. "Fine," was all she said, and she strode over to Jed's pickup and opened the passenger door to see three bags of groceries. All the while, Andy's words lingered in her head, and she watched the cousins. Whatever Jed was saying to him didn't ease her worries. In fact, as she reached for a bag of groceries, she was very aware that the next words Jed would likely say to her would be, "Time for you to go."

Secrets and lies. What the hell was going on?

Jed stared at his cousin and watched as the prettiest redhead he'd ever seen walked into his house, carrying two bags of groceries.

"Why is she here, Jed?" Andy said. "You need to hear me on this: She's trouble. Get rid of her." This was a side of Andy he didn't see often, but he was seeing it now.

"You don't come into my place, on my land, and tell me who I can or can't see," Jed said. "If it's all the same to you, Andy, I think it's time for you to leave."

His cousin was watching the open door to his house, which Diana, a woman he knew nothing about, had just walked through. "You're making a mistake, Jed. She's working some angle to get to me through you."

"Give me some credit, Andy. It sounds like you and your dad crossed a lot of lines. You want to tell me what you did?"

Andy shook his head, his face hard. Jed was seeing a side of his cousin that he'd suspected was there, but now he had more questions than answers. Andy lifted his hands in the air, walked over to his pickup, slid behind the wheel, and backed up, and as he pulled up beside Jed, he slid his window down.

"You're my cousin, Jed," he said. "You know what a bad seed is? Don't say I didn't warn you." Then he rolled his window up and drove away, leaving a trail of dust.

Jed walked over to his pickup and reached for the last bag on the seat, then closed the door and started toward his small bungalow, seeing the endless repairs he still needed to get to. As he stepped up on the crate and into the house, he spotted Diana stuffing a carton of milk into the fridge in the old, cluttered boxlike kitchen. He dumped the bag onto the small table, which had two rickety old chairs and was covered with a pile of old books and some empty bottles he hadn't cleared away. He took in the big eyes staring up at him and the tension that lingered.

"Hope everything is there," he said. "The girl working said she was pretty sure this was everything you'd picked out." Jed still couldn't understand the hate for Diana.

"Do you want me to leave?" she said. He wondered what she was hiding. There was a sharpness in her tone that he hadn't expected.

"I *want* to know what the hell that was about. Why does my cousin have it out for you? You used to live here? Never seen him go after someone like that. Is he right? Did you come back here to settle some score? Are you involved in something illegal? Seriously, Diana, you bringing drugs here? That's a few questions, to start, but I can tell you I have a lot more."

He didn't know what to make of her. She was lovely, but he didn't have a clue who she was. Could it be possible that any of what his cousin said was true?

"I'm not a drug dealer," she said. "But my mother was, among other things and whatever she was doing with Todd Friessen. When I was just a kid, I lived here. We lived in an old house she got from Todd, on property the Friessens owned. She was one of his playthings or whatever you want to call it. Faye was all about Todd, every night, every day, every moment, from what I remember. She wasn't much of a mother. The cupboards were always empty, and there were more parties, drugs, and booze than there was food for us. That was what I grew up with until the night Andy burned us out. Am I responsible for what she did? If you want to search my bag, it's already packed in my cabin. I have no drugs." She sounded calm, but he could see how shaken she was.

"No, you're not responsible for your mother, but you are responsible for yourself and the choices you make. I'm not interested in searching through your things, Diana. I just want the damn truth." He wondered how much of her story was a lie.

She took a shaky breath. "I need to know if I should be worried that you'll toss everything of mine out on a whim," she said. "Because if that's where this is headed, I'd sooner leave on my own than be treated the way I was. I didn't deserve to be treated that cruelly, and I wouldn't appreciate it now. I paid for the cabin for five days, for lessons…" She gestured to him and stopped talking, and he didn't know what he was seeing, vulnerability, fear, a fighter.

"Answer me this," he said. "Do you still see your mother? Is she a part of your life? You said she's in jail."

She didn't look away. Sadness lingered in those sky-blue eyes, as if she carried the weight of the world. "The night Andy burned us out, my mother drove us to Portland. She pulled into a bar at the edge of town and told me to stay put, left me and my little sister in the darkened parking lot. She said she needed to make some money. She walked into a bar with pills and weed, and as I said, she was arrested for selling to some undercover cop. I never saw her again. She was given ten years, and that was fifteen years ago. She never reached out, and neither did I. I have no idea where she is, nor do I want to know."

Jed sighed. "That's a hard story, Diana. No way should a kid ever have to live like that. I'm sorry about your little sister."

Diana looked away and shrugged. He couldn't imagine what she'd been through. She said, "You never answered me, Jed, about throwing me out."

"And you never answered me about why you're really here. Is it about revenge?"

She let out a heavy sigh and shook her head.

"Your silence says a lot, Diana. But hear me on this: Nobody tells me what to do on my land. This is my place. Whatever issues my cousin has with you, they stay off this land. I won't throw you out. You paid for a place and for lessons, and I always honor my word. You won't be threatened here again. But I can't help wondering why you'd come to a place where you're not wanted. I'm not a fool, Diana. Hearing what happened out there, and you being just a kid, that's a lot of anger to be carrying. Why are you really here?"

Her mouth was tight, stubborn, he thought. He could see her thinking. She shut her eyes and then flicked them open, watching him, filled with fire, passion, a lot of emotion. "You want to know why I'm really here?" she said. "Because that night changed my life forever. I'm damn angry, but more than that, I came back for justice for my little sister, who didn't have a voice. She's six feet under because of a war between Andy, Todd, and my mother, one she and I were caught in the middle of."

CHAPTER
Thirteen

The sun was up on the horizon, and Diana stood at Jed's kitchen window, waiting for the toaster. Jed had just walked out of the barn with a wheelbarrow full of manure. He'd said nothing else to her since what she'd blurted out in anger and frustration. She knew better. In fact, it had been rather stupid to tip her hand, and she still wondered whether Jed would share any of what she'd said with Andy.

The toaster popped, and Diana reached for both pieces, burning her fingers. She quickly buttered them and then spread peanut butter on both before cramming a piece in her mouth. Her cell phone rang, and she yanked it from her back jeans pocket, seeing one bar of service. She didn't recognize the number. "Hello?"

"Is this Diana Fulton, the lawyer?" a woman whispered softly on the other end.

Diana didn't move. There was no cell service out by her SUV, and she watched Jed through the kitchen window, still hauling out that wheelbarrow filled with manure. "Uh, yes, this is Diana Fulton. What can I do for you?"

"I don't know if you can help me, but I saw your flyer at the post office and, well, I'm finding myself in need of a lawyer."

Diana had peanut butter on her fingers, and there was no paper towel, so she flicked on the tap and rinsed them off. She glanced to the door and started for it, but she didn't have a clue where cell service started and ended.

"That's great," she said. "I don't have an office, so I'm kind of a mobile service at the moment. Can you tell me a little bit about the problem?"

"I'd rather not do this over the phone," the woman said. "There's a man I've been involved with, and he's decided it's time for me to go. I guess I want to know what my rights are and if you can do anything for me."

Diana needed a pen, a piece of paper. She spotted one on the cluttered table along with the folded-up paper bag. "Well, how about I come to you and see what I can do? Just let me grab a pen. Sorry, cell service where I am is spotty." She set the phone down beside her toast and hurried to the table, where she grabbed the pen and ripped off a piece of the brown paper bag. She hurried back and picked up her phone. "What is your name and address?"

"My name is Bonnie. Thanks, Miss Fulton."

"Diana. My name is Diana." She scribbled down the address, which she knew was close to the edge of town. "Just one question. Is this a boyfriend or husband? Is this a divided property?" This could be anything, but it was a job, and one she needed.

"Well, actually, a boyfriend—or rather, I'm the mistress of a very wealthy man."

Diana put down the pen, staring at the window with an odd feeling settling in. "Would I know this man, by any chance?"

There was silence for a second. "If you're from around here. I may as well just say it. It's Todd Friessen. I hope the next words out of your mouth aren't that you're sorry, but you can't help me. I know the Friessens control just about everyone, and any lawyer here would never go after them."

Diana's heart thudded. A familiar anger came out of nowhere. "I wouldn't do that," she said. "I'll see you in about an hour." Then she hung up, holding her cell phone, staring at the name and address, for a moment feeling as if justice were being handed to her. This was a chance to take a chunk out of Todd Friessen. "Okay, Diana, keep your head together," she reminded herself.

She took another bite of toast. Jed Friessen was again leading a horse out of a stall. As she finished her breakfast, she tried to organize her thoughts.

After, she strode out of the kitchen and the house and hurried over to her cabin, where she changed into lightweight slacks and a plain shirt. She slipped on her flats and gave her wavy hair a good brushing, then reached for her laptop case on the bunk, on top of the sleeping bag, and hurried out to her SUV. She had stuck her laptop in the back and just closed the door when she spotted Jed walking her way, having tied two horses to the corral.

"Where are you off to?" he said. "I have the horses ready for another lesson."

"Sorry, Jed. I just got a call from someone in town in

need of a lawyer. I'm going to meet with her. Would you be okay if we changed the lesson to this afternoon?"

Jed glanced away, his plaid shirt covered in sweat and dirt, with the sleeves rolled up to his elbows. The ends of his curly brown hair stuck out from under his hat, damp and a little too long. He gave a nod. "That's fine," was all he said, then walked back over to the corral, untied both horses, and led them in.

Diana didn't know what to make of Jed. He was a Friessen, yet he didn't act like one. As she slid behind the wheel and started her SUV, taking in the quarter tank of gas, she found herself wondering how Jed fit into the Friessen family.

She wondered if it was because of Jed that she was seeing the sign for North Lakewood differently. She spotted the gas station at the edge of town and pulled in, reaching for her wallet. She stepped out just as an older man with thick glasses, wearing a blue mechanic's jump-suit covered in grease, came out from inside, wiping his hands. The way he watched her gave her that uneasy feeling again, the one she'd managed to shake at Jed's.

"Hi, can you fill it up?" she said.

He made a face and let his gaze linger. "Would never have believed it," he said. "I heard the daughter of Faye Claremont was back."

"Just the gas, please," she said and tucked her wallet under her arm.

The man was shaking his head. "If it's all the same to you, missy, I'd just as soon you take your business elsewhere."

"Are you serious? I'm almost out of gas. Why?" she breathed out, furious. The handle for the gas pump was right there, but he was now standing in her way.

"Your mother owes me. You going to square up her debts?"

Diana didn't have a clue what to say. What else had her mother done? "I'm not my mother, and I haven't seen her," she said, though she was thinking, *And I've paid enough already.*

The man shook his head again. "You know, I don't take kindly to being burned, so I'd appreciate it if you'd move on and not come back. The thing is, missy, you say you're not your mother, but unfortunately, you look too much like her. You move on, you hear? Get on out." He actually waved his hand.

She knew if she pushed it, the next call could be to the sheriff, more trouble she didn't need. "Fine," she bit out. She pulled open her SUV and climbed in.

She had known it wouldn't be easy, coming back, but she'd had no idea just how deep the hatred was. The man she didn't remember was watching her as she checked Bonnie's address, only a few blocks away. Her gas tank was now below the quarter marker, another reminder of the importance of being prepared.

She pulled up in front of a small white bungalow at the edge of town. It was nothing fancy, but it was neat and tidy, with a white picket fence and baskets everywhere filled with vibrant red, purple, and pink flowers.

Diana retrieved her briefcase from the back, feeling the boot once again on her neck. She had to remind herself to shake it off as she strode up the steps and gave two solid knocks, probably a little louder than necessary. She made herself blow out a breath as a woman with shoulder-length blond hair who was not much older than her opened the door.

"Oh, hello, Diana?"

"Yes, I am. You must be Bonnie?"

"I am, thank you. Come in, please." The woman smiled brightly, flashing a nice set of white teeth.

Diana stepped into a warm and cozy living room filled with greens and yellows, tastefully decorated, with big, fluffy pillows on the sofa and loveseat. She heard the door close behind her.

"Don't worry about your shoes," Bonnie said. "Come in and sit." She gestured to the living room, and Diana strode over to the loveseat and sat down, putting her briefcase on the floor at her feet. "Can I get you a coffee? I just put on a pot, or I could make some tea?"

Diana reached in her bag and pulled out a pad of paper and a pen. "No, thank you. I'm fine. Why don't you sit down and explain your situation, and I'll see what I can do to help? When you called, you said you were involved with Todd Friessen and that you've ended things with him."

Bonnie sat down in an easy chair across from her. She wore black capris and a pink sleeveless shirt, and she had a curvy figure. Her eyes were a soft shade of brown, and she had freckles. "No, he decided we were done. It came in a message from his son. I have a store, a candy store in the big mall, but Todd put me up there, and he owns the inventory, the place. It was mine, but now I've been told to go. I guess everything was fine while he was sleeping with me the last two years, even though he's married. That's how Todd is. He stays married and keeps a mistress. I don't know. I figured one day maybe he'd leave her, but all the while I knew I was playing with fire. I just didn't expect to get burned so quickly."

She glanced away, and for a moment, Diana could feel her shame. Bonnie linked her fingers. "I'm sure you're thinking, how could I take up with a married man, as if I have no self-respect?"

Diana wondered a lot of things about what could make a woman take up with a man who was married to another. Maybe just hearing what Bonnie had to say would help her understand why her mother had done what she had. "I'm not here to judge you, Bonnie. I'm just here to see if I can help."

Bonnie tossed Diana an easy smile and nodded. "I was hoping the rumors were true."

Diana felt that unease again. "What rumors?"

"That a young woman showed up in town, a lawyer, and her mother was once one of Todd's mistresses. The story in town is she had some kids, and Todd and Andy burned them out, sent them packing. You know, maybe you would understand how I feel, being tossed away like garbage and having to deal with Andy—who, by the way, is the one who walked into my store with security and walked me off the property. He told me to pack up and get the hell out of town, that his father was done with me."

Diana just stared in horror. She wasn't about to talk about her personal life and what had happened. "You said this was your store. Is it in your name?"

She shook her head. "I told Andy it was my store when he showed up, but he said I was wrong, that his father wasn't that stupid. Everything set up on paper was in the Friessen name, including the contracts with suppliers."

Diana was scribbling notes down. "Did you ever sign a lease?"

Bonnie appeared puzzled, then slowly shook her head.

"Did you purchase the stock in the store? Was any of it in your name? Do you have receipts from your suppliers?" Diana tapped her pen on the pad of paper balanced on her knees.

Again, Bonnie shook her head.

"Did you have any agreement in writing with Todd?"

"No. I trusted him. I put the orders in, and all the suppliers sent the invoices to him. He had his secretary set up everything in the store, and he gave the store to me." Bonnie shrugged again. Maybe she was realizing how dire her situation was, as her eyes now took on a hint of sadness.

"Bonnie, how did you get paid?" Diana said. "I mean, this is a really nice little house you have, and the way you've furnished and decorated it couldn't have been cheap. Did you collect a salary from the shop, or did Todd give you money? Who pays for this house?" She knew she was coming across quite harshly, but Bonnie had already said Andy had told her to get out of town.

Bonnie frowned and flushed before responding. "Well, it was my store. I kept all the money made from sales. Todd would tease me and call it my 'mad money.' This house was paid for by him. I wasn't an employee, but I thought you would understand more than anyone. After all, your mama was once kept by Todd before he let Andy toss you all out. Todd's always done this. He has Andy go in and clean up after him when he's done with a woman, running her out of town. Now, don't go looking at me like that, because I didn't set my sights on Todd. It was the other way around. There's something about him..."

She sounded so defensive. "I knew something was off, because for weeks now I've barely seen him. He's pulled away, stopped coming over. You hear people say you know when a man has moved on. I never understood that until now. He's moved on. He has someone else."

Diana squeezed her pen, wondering how a woman could let a man treat her this way. She found herself thinking of Jed and how different he seemed. "And this house, is it yours?"

Bonnie shook her head. "Todd bought it for me. It's in his name."

Diana nodded. "Okay, back to your store. You took money from the cash register and didn't deposit it in the bank but in your own pocket?"

Bonnie flushed and nodded again.

"You didn't pay taxes?"

Bonnie's eyes widened. She seemed to have trouble swallowing. She slowly shook her head. "I messed up, didn't I?"

"Well, let's put it this way: From what you've told me, you're simply a guest in Todd's house. You have no legal rights to this place, as you're not his wife or common-law partner. He lives with his wife at another residence. You have no documentation that shows he's given this house to you. You don't pay rent, so rental laws won't protect you. You are, in fact, trespassing. If he chooses to sic the law on you and toss you out, you'll have no legal grounds to stand on. The burden of proof is on you, unless you have witnesses who'll come forward on your behalf?"

Diana could see how this young woman didn't have much of a leg to stand on. She was at the mercy of

Andy and Todd, two men Diana didn't believe she'd ever forgive for how they had destroyed her life.

"No one will stand up to Todd or Andy, not for me," Bonnie said. "What am I going to do?"

Diana realized this was one of the reasons she'd come back. The law was clearly on Todd's side, but this was morally reprehensible, and it seemed as if nothing had changed from fifteen years earlier. "Bonnie, I'm going to be honest with you. With everything in Todd's name, he has the law on his side. One of the things I fear is that the candy shop could be a problem. You're taking money, as you said, straight from the cash register, and Todd could argue theft and have you arrested unless you have something in writing that said it was okay. But at the same time, if he doesn't have you set up on payroll as an employee, he could also be in trouble. If he wanted to make things bad for you, he could. My suggestion is that you need to move on. Leave town. Todd is a dog, and you can't change him. You're just a notch on his bedpost, and that's all women are to him. You can't force a man to love you or commit to you. I do sympathize. With what he's doing, well, there should be a law to protect women from men like Todd Friessen." *And Andy,* she thought but didn't say.

"But I don't have any money," Bonnie said. "I didn't save anything. I'm sure you're thinking that was foolish, and I'm kicking myself now, but I never expected to be cast aside. I really thought he cared about me, loved me. How could someone who loves you do this?"

Diana found herself looking around the living room, toward the front door, wondering whether Andy would walk right through it and throw Bonnie out. "I think you answered your own question. I understand how much it hurts, but all I can suggest is that maybe I can work out a peaceful settlement with Andy, enough that you can have a new start somewhere else."

"I don't want to move. I love this house." Bonnie gripped the arms of the chair, and Diana could hear her fear, fear of the unknown. The woman was still very much in love with Todd Friessen.

"I'm going to give you some tough love, Bonnie. It may not seem like it right now, but staying here after what Todd has done is going to be like pouring salt in the wound. Let me get you a settlement so you can get the hell away from him before he destroys you."

There was something about Bonnie that made Diana sure she wasn't hearing what she was saying. Maybe she wasn't ready to let go, but she was well on her way to being burned, badly.

"You know, Diana, I heard about your mother," Bonnie said. "The gossips like to talk here. Todd has a reputation, and maybe some folks enjoy sharing it to see my reaction. A few have pointed out the long line of mistresses he has. But everyone here has heard about Faye, the famous Faye, who drugged Todd one night and stole money from his wallet like a common thief. They wonder why he didn't have her tossed in jail. Maybe I expected you to want to fight a little harder for women like us, who are used and tossed aside…"

"Whoa, I'll stop you right there," Diana said. "Women like us? Sorry, I'm not messing around with a married man, especially not one with a reputation like Todd Friessen. You went into this naively, but you've evidently figured him out, and you know he's not a good person. Don't compare me to you or my mother. Did I deserve what happened to me? I was just a kid, Bonnie. I wasn't a man's mistress." Diana stuffed her pad of paper back in her briefcase, along with her purse, and started to the door.

"Wait, don't go," Bonnie said. "Please, Diana, I thought you would be the one person who would understand what it's like to be bullied by a Friessen. It's not okay, what they're doing."

Diana paused as she pulled open the door, taking in the wide-eyed panic, the desperation. "You're right. It's not, Bonnie. It's not okay. But you seem to misunderstand who I am. I'm not like you, and I'm not my mother. Please don't confuse me for her. My advice? Todd's done you a favor. Maybe you won't see it right now, but getting away from him is a blessing. I recognize you're drowning, though, and you'll grab on to anything to keep from going under, even at another's expense. I believe in right and wrong, in fair play and honesty. If you change your mind and want me to see if I can get you a settlement, call me."

She let her gaze linger on a woman who reminded her of her mother, with her tunnel vision of Todd. Then she stepped out of the house without another word, walked down to her SUV, and pulled open the door and slid behind the wheel.

What was it about Todd Friessen that attracted women in droves? She remembered the night they'd left, and she stared back at the bungalow, seeing Bonnie in the window, watching her. Had her mother really drugged Todd? Diana wondered for a second whether, just maybe, she needed to heed her own advice. Then she gave her head a shake.

"This is different. This is for Louisa," she said to her image in the rearview mirror.

But she couldn't shake the sinking feeling, as she pulled away from the curb and turned back onto the highway, heading back to Jed's ranch, aware of her nearly empty tank of gas, that just maybe, under the rocks she was determined to overturn would be secrets the folks of North Lakewood didn't want exposed, and then there would be no going back.

Fourteen

Jed looked up as he finished digging out a rotted post on the other side of the barn. He saw the dust from Diana's SUV before he heard it. He found himself aware of her, yet there was so much about her that he didn't understand. Why had she come back to a place where something horrible had happened? He'd never forget her face, her sorrow over the little sister she'd lost at the hands of fate.

Then there was his uncle, Todd, and his cousin, Andy, and their part in this shitshow.

He waited for her to park and ran the back of his hand over his forehead, wiping away the sweat, feeling grungy. Diana climbed out of her SUV, dressed plain and casual in flats and tan slacks, which did nothing to hide her beauty.

"So how'd it go?" he called out, still wondering why she'd insisted on setting up a practice there.

"Enlightening, but a waste of time," Diana said. "She's one of Todd Friessen's mistresses, and he's done with her and has tossed her aside. She hasn't a leg to stand on. It seems she wanted to use what happened to my mother to her advantage. I'm not a liar or a cheat, and I'm kind of pissed that she thought I would be. At the same time, yeah, she's getting screwed. I don't understand why so many women just hand their power over to a man and believe everything is going to be okay. She's hurting; I get it, I really do, more than anyone, but I don't like that people think I'm like Faye. I had to grow up with that shit, not knowing who would be in the house when I got up in the morning or whether I could go to school and leave my little sister with a woman who was passed out, drunk."

Jed rested his shovel against the barn. In the depth of Diana's blue eyes was her vulnerability, peeled back just a bit. "So my uncle is at it again, is he? What happened?" He pulled off his leather gloves and set them on the rail post by the barn. Todd had never been a man of virtue, and Jed had never understood why he stayed married to a woman he didn't love. Everything about Todd was messy, even though it appeared otherwise.

"I'm sure you've heard about Todd's mistress and the candy store," she said. "I was in town only five minutes before the post office lady filled me in. Well, apparently, she's the client being sent packing."

Jed only shook his head. He'd never been one to pay any mind to the gossips, but he was aware of who Todd was and what he did with his wealth and position. Even Andy seemed to control so much of that part of the state. "Yeah, I heard about her. So she's the one? Well, if you want peace, Diana, taking a case like that isn't going to give it to you. Wise choice, walking away."

He wasn't sure what to make of the way she was looking at him now.

"Seriously?" she said. "Walking away because of Andy and Todd's shenanigans is not what I did. In fact, I offered to work out some type of settlement. She is owed, but all I did was point out that the law isn't on her side and she needs to work with what she has. She didn't want to hear it. Make no mistake, I'm not giving those two predators a pass."

He felt the bite in her words, the anger.

"I realize they're your family," she continued.

"Don't put me in their camp, Diana," he said. "I have eyes and can see, and I don't condone anything they've done to hurt people. But at the same time, two wrongs don't make a right."

Passion oozed from this woman, and maybe that was why he felt so damn unsettled around her. She was still holding on to something, pissed, angry, and she let out a sigh of frustration.

"I need to get some gas," she said. "I'm almost out and just made it back, but I need to head to Marysville and fill up. Do you maybe have a full gas can around here? I don't think I have enough in the tank to make it all the way there."

He found himself looking over to her SUV, knowing his jerry can of gasoline was only half full. "Sure, but why go all the way out there?" he said. "Fill up in North Lakewood. It's closer." And why hadn't she done that before driving all the way back? Sometimes women made no sense.

She made a face. "Well, that's the thing," she said. "I stopped for gas first, but I was denied."

He stared at her.

Her blue eyes flashed with fire. "Yeah. Apparently, word has spread beyond Mr. Harris that the daughter of Faye Claremont is back in town. Everyone who had issues with my mother is making a point of telling me their doors are closed to me, the gas station manager included. No idea what Faye did, what she took from him, but he did ask if I was going to pay him back for it." She lifted her hands. He wondered what part his cousin had in this.

"Give me your keys," he said, and he held out his hand.

Diana appeared startled. Her blue eyes widened, and she stepped back. "What? Why?"

"Because I'm done with this shit," he said. She handed him her keys, and he gestured to her SUV and said, "Get in."

As Diana slid in the passenger side, he had already started the engine and was taking in the comfortable leather seats. He said, "Looks like you got enough gas here to make it, just barely." Then he pulled his door closed and put it in gear before pulling on his seatbelt, feeling how smooth the SUV was compared to his pickup.

"Jed, what are you doing? Aren't you the one who said a minute ago that I should walk away from confrontation?"

He pulled onto the highway, really giving it gas, taking in the gauge, where the light hadn't come on yet. "There is a line, Diana. Being denied gas or service crosses it. You're not your mother. This shit is getting really old." He didn't know what to make of the way she was watching him or how quiet she'd become.

"So you're fighting my battles?" she said, turning to

look straight ahead. What drove her, and why was his cousin so damn focused on driving her out of there?

"No. I'm defending you from someone who should know better."

She was unsmiling, looking out the side window but saying nothing. He spotted the edge of town, the gas station just up ahead. The gas light popped on, and he couldn't help thinking, what if she'd run out of gas on the side of the road, a woman alone? So many things could have gone wrong.

He pulled up to the pump just as the door opened, and Rex, the familiar grease monkey, was already halfway to the SUV by the time Jed got out.

The man seemed to hesitate mid-step. "Jed. Uh…?"

Jed heard the passenger door and knew Diana had stepped out.

"What are you doing with her?" Rex said.

Jed lifted the nozzle and flicked it on as he unscrewed the gas cap, then shoved it in. "Filling up Diana's SUV with gas. Apparently, you denied her, and I can't understand why you'd do something like that," he said. He'd never had a problem with the owner of the five and dime station.

"Jed, you don't know her," Rex said. "She'll rob you blind. You weren't around when she used to live here with her mother. Those Claremonts are trouble. The night they were sent packing was a good day for this community. If it weren't for her mother, my little cousin wouldn't have had his life destroyed, in and out of rehab, hooked on meth, last I heard. She started him down that path, him and many around here."

"Your cousin made that choice, Rex. You and I both know that. Understand that Diana is not her mother.

She was just a kid. No one helped her or her little sister. Her mother may have been a problem, but be careful you don't become the same to Diana. I remember what you said about your cousin, how he took all the cash from your till one day, cleaned it out. You wonder how many others he's done it to. You want to blame her mother, fine. But ask yourself how many others' lives your cousin has turned upside down."

The awkwardness lingered before Rex said, "Fine, fill it up. Gas is on me today." He moved to walk away.

"No, Diana will pay for the gas," Jed said. "Fair is fair, and when she comes to fill her car up again, you'll behave decently, because I don't think you want to start something with me."

The nozzle clicked off. Diana's blue eyes were wide, her expression spooked, as he pulled the nozzle out and screwed on the gas cap.

"Are you threatening me, Jed?"

"Rex, if I were threatening you, you'd know it. Diana, go pay for your gas."

Rex lifted a hand in the air. "Her money is no good here. Told you—"

"And I told you she's paying for her gas, and you're going to give her a damn receipt for it. Because one thing that isn't going to happen is a visit from the sheriff to cause Diana more grief with accusations that she didn't pay or that she's a thief, which she's not."

Diana raced back to the SUV and grabbed her wallet, and Rex followed her inside the station, shaking his head. Jed watched as she paid for her gas, and he took his time washing the windows. When she stepped back out, he slipped behind the wheel and started the vehicle, and after she'd got in, he put it in gear and pulled out. But instead of going home, he turned the other way.

"Jed, where are we going?"

He glanced over to her, and the way her blue eyes lingered on him, with such depth, he wanted to know more about her. "To put an end to this crap. First groceries, then gas? No, I've had it. I intend to put a stop to this, and the only way to do that is to go right to who's responsible."

He'd never had a problem with his cousin before, but something about all of this told him Andy's hand was in it.

The heat had a way of making the strong odor of cattle country more pungent. Dark clouds were beginning to gather in the distance. The scent of rain had always settled her, but Diana didn't know what to make of Jed driving her right into the lions' den, down a massive paved driveway, through the open gates of a huge estate. The house was one she'd seen only a few times from the forest in the distance, but she swore it was bigger than she'd imagined.

Jed stopped at the base of the most magnificent stone stairs she'd ever seen, turned off her SUV, and stepped out without a word. She realized he'd likely leave her sitting out there, and she couldn't have that, so she climbed out, hearing thunder in the distance. Jed took the stone steps two at a time, then opened the front door and walked in.

"What the hell are you doing here?"

Diana had taken only a step when she heard his voice. She turned to see Andy in a black cowboy hat and blue jeans, his icy blue eyes filled with anger for her. The way he walked toward her, invading her space, he would likely walk right over her. She fought the urge to step back. Jed had closed the door behind him, and she was alone outside with Andy.

"I'm not sure," she said. "Your cousin is inside. I was denied gas and told Jed, and he's pretty angry. Guess he's having a word with Todd, maybe looking for you, as well." She went to pull her arms over her chest, remembering how his eyes had lingered on her in the most inappropriate of ways. Andy dragged that shrewd gaze of his to the front door.

"One thing Faye did well was getting men to do her dirty work," he said. "She had a way about her, you know—a carefully placed lie, a story, and when those didn't work, she'd use her body. Is this the plan, Diana? Because we've been there, done that with your mother, all her games and the lives she turned upside down. Are you working it with my cousin to turn him against his family? You using that body of yours, just like your mother?"

She felt the slap and had to remind herself not to bite. Andy had done a great job of trashing her, a worthy opponent in a fight. "Does it matter what I say, Andy? It seems you've already painted me with the same brush as my mother."

His brow furrowed, and he looked intently down on her, then nodded softly. "I'm telling you again: You hurt my cousin and I'll bury you."

She lifted her chin, feeling the familiar unease churning inside her.

"I'll pay you to leave," he said. "A hundred thousand. You get in your SUV, and you drive away and never come back."

She realized he was serious. "When I leave, it will not be because you've made me. For the record, I'm not for sale, and I wouldn't take a dime from you. You keep trying to say I'm like my mother, but I think you're trying to ease your conscience after what you did to me and my sister. I don't know what my mother did to your dad, but let me tell you what my life was like, that pathetic kid you terrorized. You could have helped us, but you turned your back, standing by a man who uses women, who's despicable. All the nights my mother drank, partied, all the men she brought home, your father was there more often than not. I woke up every morning and had to clean up empty bottles, ashtrays and cigarettes, and drugs, pills, paraphernalia, never knowing who would be passed out naked on the sofa, wondering whether the box of cereal, the only food in the cupboard, would still be there, or if there would be enough left for me and my sister to eat. Then it would begin again every night. That was what I faced, and your father knew. I was a kid, Andy!"

She studied his face, seeing confusion and something else, something that betrayed the tough guy who influenced this county and its people.

"I'm not going anywhere," she said.

"I'm sorry for that kid, but you shouldn't have come back," he said. "You play the innocent well, but this was a mistake. Yeah, our fight was with your mother, but you've come back to a place you're not wanted. No one does that unless they're planning something, revenge, trouble. You seem to forget I know how it works. There are a lot of other places for you to go, but you're not staying here, Diana. One way or the other, I'll see to it that you leave."

She felt the first drop of rain, then another. She looked up to a man she'd been head over heels for as a kid and knew he meant every word he was saying. The rain fell harder, and she reached for her car door to pull it open, but his hand was right there, slapping it closed again.

"You're a desirable woman, Diana, hot, sexy, the whole package, but one way or another, you're leaving, because any threat against my family will never be allowed to stay." He pressed against her, all his hardness, his warm breath on her ear. She had to shut her eyes as he ran his hand over her breast and down.

She pushed back hard. "Don't you ever touch me like that again!" she shouted, and she yanked the door open, climbed in, and pulled it closed behind her, still feeling where he'd touched her as if he'd thought he had every right.

He was walking away, up the steps to the front door, which opened as Jed stepped out. She didn't know what passed between them before Jed ran down the steps. The rain was coming down in buckets now, and he jerked the driver's door open and climbed in with water dripping from his ratty cowboy hat. Diana reached for her seatbelt and pulled it on.

"He say something to you?" Jed said as he started the SUV and flicked on the wipers.

Diana took in the now closed door. "Warned me off, tried to pay me to leave. Thinks I'm using you to get to him." She pulled in a shaky breath, feeling the burn in her eyes, and she had to turn away, blinking hard past the hurt. When Jed ran his hand over her arm, she turned to face him, unsure of what he was thinking.

"So what happened in there?" She nodded to the massive estate, which likely had an army of servants.

"May have been wasting my breath, but I said my piece." He put the SUV in drive and splashed through the puddles, and all Diana could think as they drove back toward the highway was that she was now neck deep in a family where one cousin was good and the other was hellbent on destroying her.

Sixteen

Something about the early hours before the sun came up gave Jed so much clarity. Truth be told, he was thinking of the rundown cabin in which a woman by the name of Diana Fulton was sleeping. He knew without even looking at the calendar that she'd be gone in two more days. He should welcome it, considering the chaos that had followed her arrival, disrupting everything about his peaceful, lonely existence. But so much about her story, things his cousin and uncle had had a hand in, bothered him.

The day before, Todd had welcomed him because he was his brother's son, but Jed didn't think he'd ever forget his uncle's heavy gaze, which reminded him of a snake coiled up, ready to strike.

Jed had told him to back off and leave Diana be.

Todd had only smiled and said, "Be careful, Jed, my boy. The apple doesn't fall far from the tree with that one. She's got you fooled, and the day will come very soon that she'll take you down with her. That place of yours, the one you're building way out there from the ground up, could be gone just like that, in the blink of an eye." Todd had snapped his fingers.

Jed realized he'd never understood why Todd was the way he was. He knew Diana had no idea of the danger she was in. He stared out the window, still in the shadows, and finished off his coffee before shrugging on his coat, pulling open the door, and stepping down into the dirt, immediately splashing through a puddle.

He waited for the nicker that didn't come.

"Hey, where are you two?" he called out. It was still dark, but his horses always greeted him.

The light of the fading moon before the sun hit the horizon illuminated the gate to the corral, which was open. His gaze went right to Diana's parked SUV, then to the darkened cabin, where she would still be sleeping. He was already walking her way, feeling the wind of another day. Rain would be there soon.

He fisted his hand and pounded on her cabin door. "Diana!"

She pulled the door open, her red hair a mess, wearing only a long t-shirt above her slender legs. "What is it?"

"Were you in the corral last night with the horses?" He knew it had come out rather sharply, but he'd said more than once that the gate should never be left open.

"No," she said. "I showered and did some work on my laptop. Fell asleep not long after. Why, what's wrong?"

Something about what his uncle had said was coming back to him. This place meant everything to Jed, a place he'd bought with his own money. Everything there, he had created it with his own two hands.

"The gate is open and the horses are gone," he said. "Get dressed. I need your help."

Her expression was startled, and she nodded. "Yeah, of course." She closed the cabin door, and Jed started walking. Had she really gone to sleep, or could his uncle be right?

He strode into the barn and flicked on the outside light, which lit up the corral, just as he heard Diana walking his way. She was in blue jeans, her hiking boots, and a light brown sweater. Jed took in the muddy ground, the hoofprints of his horses and footprints that weren't his.

"You left the horses outside last night?" she said. She was right there, and he crouched down, seeing how small her feet were compared to the large boot prints.

"I'm redoing the roof above their stalls," he said. "The entire barn is in need of repair. It's not the first time they've stayed out there. You see these boot prints? I'd say from a large man, big feet, a couple different ones. You hear anyone out here last night?" He glanced up to her.

She frowned, staring at the prints in the mud, and shook her head. "No, but then, your house is closer. You didn't hear anything, either?"

What was he supposed to say, that he slept like the dead out there sometimes? He'd heard nothing at all. "Shit," he bit out. Someone was messing with him, and he'd let his uncle mess with his head about Diana. She didn't do this. There was no way she could have. "No, I heard nothing, not even the horses."

She walked over to the driveway, and he didn't know what she was looking at. "Who would do such a thing,

Jed? I take it you've had no trouble here until I showed up?"

She didn't look over to him, but he could hear it in her voice, and he was ashamed to admit that he'd considered it could have been her. Unless she was still playing him. Damn, he had to look away, furious at how his uncle's words were still stuck in his head, filling him with doubts about Diana. *She's not her mother.*

"No, I haven't, which has me wondering too many things. Right now, I need to find my horses," he said.

She stood there, looking out into the dimness. A hint of light was just hitting the horizon, and her hair was pulled back, her face pale and gorgeous. He realized he'd never felt so protective of anyone.

"It wasn't me, Jed," she said. "I would never do this, not to you. But I have a feeling it's going to be made to look like me. You know, I found something out about my mother. I don't know if it's true. When I went to see Bonnie, she said my mother drugged Todd, slipped him something. Not sure what she expected the outcome to be, but I wonder if that was why Andy came in as hard as he did. Did she try to kill him? My little sister, Louisa, and I were only collateral because we were her children."

He let his gaze linger and didn't have a clue what to say to that. "Diana, you're not your mother. If she did that, she has to pay for it, not you. I can see how it's getting to you, how you're taking it on and letting it mess with your head. I know you didn't do this, but I think you're right that someone is willing to make it look like you did. I wonder if you thought of what you'd be walking into, coming back here?"

She only shrugged, then lifted her hands helplessly

in the air. "No, I didn't expect any of this. It's as if fate changed whatever plan I had. Honestly, Jed, I got a law degree because I didn't understand why the Friessens had more rights than us because of how much money and power they had. That drove me on this path, and maybe I did come back to set the record straight or get some type of justice. Did I have a plan?" Again, she shook her head and lifted her hands, then let out a heavy sigh of frustration. "I didn't think it would be this hard, but I would never put someone innocent in the line of fire. I never expected to meet you, Jed. God damn it, I never expected to land here! I didn't come back here to find love…" She stopped talking, and he felt her awkwardness as she realized what she'd said. "I think I know who did this: Andy," she said, and licked her lips.

Would the hate between his cousin and Diana always be there? Jed found himself shaking his head. "Andy does a lot of things when cleaning up after his father, but this, here? This has Todd written all over it."

She stilled, her brows pulling together. When he started walking back to the house, she called out, "Where are you going?"

He turned to her. "To get my keys," he said. *And to pay my uncle and Andy another visit.*

The sun was fully up, and Jed still hadn't returned. Diana was on her second cup of coffee, standing in his kitchen, staring at the open corral gate, wondering why trouble was always lurking in the shadows for her. Worse, now it seemed she'd brought it right to Jed's doorstep. She shut her eyes against the ache. So many lines had been blurred, all because she hadn't expected to feel so much for Jed Friessen.

When her cell phone rang, her heart thudded. She hoped it was Jed. "Hello? This is Diana."

"Diana, this is Bonnie." It sounded as if she was crying. "I know I'm probably the last person you want to hear from, but I'm sorry for what I said. You were right about everything. I've had time to think, and I'd like to leave, if you'll help, if you'd still be willing to see whether Andy would agree to pay something in a settlement. Then I'll move on."

Her stomach knotted—disappointment? "Sure, I will. Let me talk with Andy," she said. She knew something must have happened, as Bonnie was sniffling and weeping on the other end, but there was only so far she was willing to go down the Todd and Bonnie rabbit hole.

"Thank you, Diana. I truly am sorry for what I said before. I didn't mean to be ungrateful, and I know you were just trying to help. I guess I just didn't want it to end like this, to be just another notch on Todd Friessen's bedpost, so to speak." She blew her nose.

"I understand more than you think," Diana said, "but sometimes it's our heads that get us in trouble because we refuse to see the signs right in front of us. This is what Todd does, so be smarter and move on and learn from this."

Bonnie sniffed. "Thank you, Diana. And for the record, I know whatever your mother did was pretty bad, but Andy doing what he did to you kids, that wasn't okay. There are a few other folks around here who also believe it wasn't right, but they'll never admit it. Most people would never stand up for what's right. They don't ever want to shake things up because they just want to be left alone, to work, to buy a house, to have a family, to take a holiday. They don't want to get involved in anything that might unsettle their everyday normalcy. I sure found out that no one likes to take a stand for the underdog. Most folks here just want you to go away and stop you from popping off."

Diana knew that was true, but she wasn't made that way. "Again, let me talk to Andy. How soon are you planning on leaving?"

Bonnie sighed. "Tonight. Andy was here just before I called you, all fired up…" Her voice caught, and she whimpered. "I called his house last night to try to reason with Todd, but I never talked to him. Apparently, calling the house was the one thing I was never supposed to do."

Diana winced, understanding what Bonnie had done, likely in desperation. She was reeling because she'd figured out she'd lost. "Don't worry, Bonnie. I'll get back to you before the day is out. I'll talk to Andy, but in the meantime, pack your bags."

She hung up and walked out to the simple boxy cabin, where she changed into her dark pantsuit and flats and put on a light touch of makeup, just powder and blush, so she wouldn't appear washed out. Then she brushed her long, tangled hair and tied it back into a ponytail.

She hurried to her vehicle, dodging a big puddle and the mud from all the rain. She stopped and glanced at the empty spot where Jed's truck should have been, and she wished he were there just so she could talk to him, see his smile and that damn ratty cowboy hat, or just know he was okay. Whether he had a cell phone or not she didn't have a clue, so she pulled open her back door, reached for her briefcase on the floor, and pulled out a pad of paper and a pen to scribble a note for him.

Bonnie called. She's decided to heed my advice. I'm going to meet Andy and work something out for her. Thanks for believing me. I hope you found the horses.

She hesitated only a second before scribbling her name and folding the note, then walking over to his closed front door and shoving it in the jam so he'd see it when he pulled in.

She slid in under the steering wheel and drove out, determined to at least get something for a woman who'd done the unforgivable by getting involved with the likes of Todd Friessen.

THE WINDS HAD PICKED UP, and thick, dark clouds were gathering overhead as Diana approached the estate, down the long slate-gray driveway and through the heavy iron gates to the front door. Something about driving in was unsettling. She was out of her element.

She parked beside what she knew was Andy's truck. At least he was home, which should have eased her worry about whom she'd ask for when she walked up to the door. She left her purse but tucked her cell phone in her pocket, then carried her briefcase up the wide stone steps. The wind blew strands from her ponytail as she glanced at the red roses sweeping up the north wall of the house, and she wondered how she'd missed that the day before. It was stunning, hundreds of the sweet-scented flowers.

Diana took a deep breath and pressed the doorbell beside a polished mahogany door with a stained glass insert in the center. The door alone was a showpiece. She heard the chime inside, and her heart thudded before it was opened a few seconds later, not by a servant but by Andy. She had to look way up. He was so damn tall, just like Jed. A fire seemed to ooze from Andy, one that unsettled her. She had to remind herself not to cower.

"Diana, what do you want?" He was so abrupt, and she picked up on a cruelness in the way he spoke. She wondered if it had always been there.

"I'm here as an attorney representing Bonnie Hays.

I understand you paid her a visit this morning and gave her that famous ultimatum of yours. What is it, pack your bags and be out by nightfall?" Damn, she was proud of how strong she sounded even though she was shaking inside.

"So my father's whore calls the daughter of his former whore for what, a shakedown? Is that what this is? Wow, this day just keeps getting better and better." He angled his head as she heard a vehicle, then nodded to the driveway and said, "You drag my cousin into this too?"

She turned her head so fast. Why did Andy hate her so much? It seemed to be one slap after another, but there was Jed in that damn rumpled cowboy hat and a long duster raincoat. He hurried up the steps, and she couldn't explain what a welcome sight he was.

"Got your note," he said. "You okay?"

She could only nod. "You find the horses?"

He made a face and shook his head. "No," he said. His horses were still missing, yet he had shown up there for her. She forced herself to turn back to Andy.

"I dragged no one into anything," she said.

"What's going on here, son?"

Diana jerked her gaze past Andy to a distinguished graying man who was the image of him thirty years older. He wore denim jeans, a black shirt, and a fierce, shrewd look that had Diana swallowing the heavy lump suddenly jammed in her throat. Her memories from so long ago threatened to turn her into that scared little girl as he stared at her, hard, unforgiving. Todd was a man she really wouldn't want to be alone with, and she didn't understand why women flocked to him.

"Jed, you bring this piece of trash to my doorstep?" he said.

She felt Jed's hand on her arm. "Careful, Todd," he drawled, and she didn't miss the warning.

An odd smile pulled at the corners of Todd's lips.

"Todd Friessen," Diana said, "as I was saying to Andy, I'm a lawyer representing Bonnie Hays, your mistress, the one you decided you're done with and want driven from town. I'm here to work out a settlement for her, and then she'll go peacefully."

She was aware of Jed standing right beside her, having her back. She had to remind herself this was real. His hand touched her back as if he knew what she was thinking.

"A lawyer? Amazing," Todd said.

The wind was picking up, and Andy finally stepped back and gestured inside. "Come in and let's settle this," was all he said.

Diana turned to Jed, who gestured and followed her inside, then closed the door behind them. She took in the massive staircase, the tiled floor, and what looked like a front library or office with a fireplace, sofa, and bar. She walked side by side with Jed and squeezed the handle of her briefcase, reminding herself to breathe.

"I think you're a little out of your element, missy," Todd said to her. Andy had gone to stand in front of the large mahogany desk and pulled his arms across his chest.

"Dad, enough, already," he said rather sharply. "You want to settle this? The house isn't hers. The store isn't hers. The only things that are hers are the clothes on her back. She leaves. Now we're settled." Andy was very direct, abrupt. Jed shook his head.

"Andy," Diana said, "when you show up tonight with your cowboys to throw her out, I'll be waiting with a news crew and cameras. We'll be sure the video goes viral across the internet and is broadcast to every station in the state, showing big, powerful thugs tossing a woman out into the street because your father is on to mistress number…fifty, or is it sixty?"

Todd actually laughed from where he leaned against the fireplace mantel. "No news station would run it," he said. "You may get a camera there and some lowly reporter wanting to make a name, but I guarantee you no station will ever air it. You forget how information is controlled? Nice try, though."

She lifted her chin, knowing he was right. "Doesn't matter. It could be just one camera and the post would still go viral. It'll hurt, maybe even get back to your wife."

He flashed those dark eyes her way. He was not a man she could play games with. "Oh, you don't want to be doing that, or you'll find yourself hurt in ways you can't imagine."

"Do not threaten Diana again, Todd," Jed said. "I already warned you once."

Diana dragged her gaze to him, then back to Todd. "Todd, you've hurt a lot of women, but maybe I need to tell just one story: mine. You know how you used my mother? She was your plaything. Where did she fall, mistress number five or ten? Doesn't matter. You and your son tossed her and her children out into the dead of night because you were done with them. You ignored the plight of me and my sister and left two helpless kids in the clutches of a drug-dealing whore. Isn't that what you called her? By the way, she was arrested for dealing and given ten years in prison the very night you tossed her children out instead of getting them help. Don't you think people will question why you didn't call the authorities for her children or why one of them is dead? My sister, Louisa, was only four years old, and she died because of that night. You may come out and say your hands are clean, but it was too messy."

"Sounds like you're threatening me, telling stories. I'll sue you for slander."

"Slander? Like how you've done your best, both you and your son, to destroy my name, alluding to the possibility that I'm a drug-dealing whore like my mother?"

There was silence. Todd didn't pull his gaze as he said, "What do you want, Diana?"

"I want you to stop bullying women, messing with their lives, turning them upside down." She leaned in.

Todd only laughed.

Jed's hand was on her again. "Diana…" he said, and she didn't miss the warning.

She couldn't change who Todd was, but she shook her head and glanced over to Andy. "So who's the next victim going to be?"

Andy pulled his hand over his face and shook his head. "You've made your point, Diana. What is it you want, exactly?"

"No, you are *not* going to negotiate—not with her!" Todd shouted.

Diana instinctively stepped back, bumping into Jed. His hand slid around her. She had to remind herself she was strong, but something about Todd really terrified her. How could her mother have been involved with the likes of him? Then again, she didn't understand anything about her mother, since Faye hadn't known how to be one.

Andy said nothing. In fact, it appeared he was waiting for Diana to give him an answer.

"Bonnie is prepared to leave, but she needs a month to find another place to live and to arrange for movers to move her things out," she said. "She needs a fair settlement for the loss of her store and income and for how your father used her."

Andy chuckled, but it was in no way pleasant. He glanced away. "Just give me a fucking number and stop with the games."

"Forty thousand and she's gone for good."

Andy shook his head, his lips forming a thin white line. "Twenty, she signs a non-disclosure, and she's gone by nightfall."

"Thirty, she agrees to your confidentiality agreement, and she leaves in a week." Diana was shaking inside but hoped she appeared cool and confident.

"Done," Andy snapped, his arms pulled over his chest. Diana had to remind herself they still weren't finished. He strode around the large desk, and she took a second to really see the deep red carpets, the oil paintings on the walls. Everything in this place cost more than she'd ever see in this lifetime. Andy had yanked open a drawer and pulled out a checkbook, which he tossed on the desk before flicking his gaze over to her.

"Well, this is what you asked for," Jed said in a low voice. She glanced over to him and nodded before taking one step and another over to the desk.

Todd's gaze was burning into her, but then he walked to the bar, uncapped a decanter of amber liquid, and poured three fingers into a glass before tossing an ice cube in. "You heard from your mama?" he said, and he was looking right at her with eyes that had her wondering whether the man felt anything for anyone.

"No. I haven't seen her since the night you forced us out fifteen years ago. She was arrested for selling dope to an undercover cop."

Todd grunted, then let out a rough laugh after downing the drink and setting it on the bar. She didn't know what he was thinking about her mother or any of this. "Andy," he said, "make sure this is wrapped up today, and have our lawyers make sure Miss Claremont sticks to what's agreed, no monkeying around."

"That's Miss Fulton," Diana stated rather abruptly.

The odd expression on Todd's face lingered for a second. Then he gave his head a shake, turned, and left without saying another word.

"You know, cousin, this overprotective role you've got going on is touching, but ease up," Andy said. "I'm not going to hurt her."

"What the hell are you doing, Andy, cleaning up after your father, his mess? How long've you been doing this? How many women have you done this to?"

She hadn't expected this from Jed, but Andy never flinched. "Jed, please," she said, seeing he was only one step from doing something for her. Damn, she was truly sunk. "Jed," she said again, then nudged him. He flicked his gaze down to her and nodded.

"Diana, whether you believe it or not, I don't think you deserved what happened to you as a kid," Andy said. "If I could go back, I'd call social services and make sure you and your sister were taken away from Faye. I am not a monster, but your mother was, and that's the God-honest truth. She was not a good person."

She already knew that, but neither was Todd, and Andy's hands weren't clean in any of this, either. Instead of continuing any talk of Faye Claremont, Diana said, "Well, come on, Andy. Let's finish this agreement, and then this will be one less problem you have to take care of. Jed, you don't need to stay. Remember the horses? You need to find them."

Andy said nothing. He took in her and Jed with an odd, confused look. "What happened to the horses?"

Jed shook his head. "Someone showed up in the wee hours and let my horses out. Figure a couple of big guys on horseback, from the tracks I could find." There was an edge to his voice.

Diana didn't know what to make of Andy's expression, concerned or something.

Jed said, "As soon as you finish this with my cousin, then we'll leave."

Andy gestured to a chair in front of his desk, "Well, sit down. As you said, let's finish this."

Eighteen

Diana stood outside Bonnie's small house, holding the printed agreement she'd hashed out with Andy. The only problem was that the signed check was sitting on Andy's desk and would be given to Bonnie only when she signed the agreement. Jed had parked his truck behind hers. The wind had picked up, heralding a cold and rainy fall. Gone were the hot days of summer.

"You didn't have to follow me, Jed," she said. "The horses…"

He walked over to her. He needed to shave, and there was something rugged about this man, who seemed prepared to fight every one of her battles for her. No one had ever done that for her before. Maybe that was why her chest ached so much.

"When you're dealing with the likes of Andy and Todd, I think I do," he said, and she nodded. "You need her to sign. Come on."

She gripped the agreement and the pen and started up the steps, then knocked on the door, and Bonnie pulled it open, wearing a blue sweater, and her gaze went right to Jed. Diana said, "Bonnie, I got an agreement. I need you to sign it. As soon as you do, Andy will turn the check over." She handed the agreement to Bonnie, who appeared startled.

She took it and lifted a page. "Could I have a minute to read it? Are you sure this is for the best?"

Diana was still standing on the doorstep, and she felt the indecisiveness, a hesitation, as if Bonnie might not sign.

"Bonnie, is it?" Jed cut in. "Todd's not interested in you. Sign it, and by next week he won't remember your name. Take the money and go. Start a new life. Diana went to bat for you, so don't drag this out. Just sign it, already."

Bonnie stared at Jed, wide-eyed. Diana held out the pen to her, and she hesitated only a second before walking to a small entry table inside and scribbling her name. She flicked the pen and held it back out.

"This is for the best, Bonnie," Diana said. "I'll take this to Andy and be back with your check. It will be enough to get you started somewhere else. This is a good thing." She started down the steps with Jed.

"Maybe for you," Bonnie called out. "But Todd's the only man I've ever loved."

Diana found herself looking back. A tear slid down Bonnie's cheek, which she roughly wiped away. Then she closed the door without another word.

Diana headed to her SUV. Jed's beat-up rusty brown pickup was parked behind it. "Jed, you don't have to babysit me. I appreciate your coming along, but I'm a big girl. I can take care of myself, and you need to be looking for the horses."

"Diana, I never said this, but the minute the horses were gone, my first thought was that it was you," Jed hadn't looked at her as he said it, but now he did, and knowing he'd thought that way of her hurt more than anything. "Maybe I shouldn't have said anything, but I realized those were the words my uncle had said, that trouble follows you, as if he were trying to warn me. But if there's one thing I do well, it's read horses and people. I'm embarrassed that I let Todd get in my head. So yeah, I needed to show up, because you walked right into the lions' den, and, law degree or not, Diana, you were in over your head."

She didn't know what to say. "You thought I would do that to you?" she said. "I love you, Jed. I guess that's the difference; I never expected to fall in love with you." She made herself look away. "Go look for your horses. I need to finish this."

She didn't wait for him to say anything as she slid behind the wheel and started her SUV, then watched as Jed Friessen, a man she'd never planned to feel so much for, climbed in his truck, wheeled it around, and headed back the other way.

"SHE SIGNED IT, Andy. Honor your end of the agreement." Diana stood in the middle of the library where she'd been not even an hour earlier. She had noticed so many other fine details of the home, the wainscoting on the trim, the rock fireplace with colors that were completely balanced, stones that appeared individually placed, leather chairs positioned just so, and wall-to-wall books that appeared perfectly aligned. The

room was warm with greens and gold, a sharp contrast
to the deep red carpet.

"Would you like a drink, Diana, a glass of wine?"
Andy poured himself one from a crystal decanter at the
stocked bar. As they had entered the room, the last thing
she'd expected was to be sharing a drink with Andy or
having a civil one-on-one.

"No, thank you. I don't drink."

He stared at her for a second with an odd look.

"Andy, if you just hand over the check, I'll be on my
way." She gestured to his desk, where the signed agreement had been placed.

Andy dangled his glass, then swallowed. He set it
down on the smoothly polished desk with a clatter.
"Diana, maybe I was wrong and you're not like your
mother."

She wondered if this was an apology. She didn't
know what to make of the way he was watching her. He
didn't move over to the desk, and she didn't see the
check sitting where it had been when she left.

"I'm trying to apologize, Diana," he said. "You
could give me that, at least."

The way he said it, she realized his ego was staring
her down, not about to make anything easy for her.
She let out a heavy sigh. "Of course, by all means,
apologize, but let's be clear on what you're apologizing
for. Is it my little sister, who never saw her fifth birth-
day, the fact your father was a part of whatever my
mother was doing, or the fact that you did your best to
drive me out of town and see to it that the folks here
wouldn't give me a chance? Faye Claremont was a
shitty mother, but she was all I had, and I didn't know
anything else. Your anger was with her, but my sister

and I were collateral. Is that what you're apologizing for?"

He said nothing, just took one step over to her, then another until he was standing right in front of her. He was tall, just like Jed, but nothing like him. "I don't want my cousin hurt," he said. "Don't mess with him."

She had to look away and shut her eyes. "Just give me the damn check, Andy, and I'll leave."

He didn't move, only angled his head. Why was he looking at her the way he was, with too much interest, too much something? "You're the most beautiful woman I've ever seen, Diana. Are you sleeping with him?"

"What does it matter?"

He shut his eyes for a second, then walked away, around the desk, and opened the top drawer to pull out the check. He held it out to her. "Will you be leaving town?"

Another question she didn't want to answer. "I don't know, Andy. Right now, I'm helping a woman get a new start." And then there was Jed, a man she'd never expected to feel so much for. She took the check from him.

"Jed has nothing but a rundown piece-of-shit property he'd be better off bulldozing," Andy said. "He scrapes by. I see it, we all see it. He makes his money with those damn horses, taking people on pack trips, setting up camp all summer. He chops wood in the winter, teaches riding lessons. What I'm saying, Diana, is he has nothing to offer you."

Diana took in the room, feeling the enormity of the mansion, so big that she had no idea how many rooms it had. She figured the painting on the wall, by an artist she'd never heard of, was worth more than Jed would ever make. "That's where you're wrong, Andy. Jed is one of the most decent, honorable men I've ever met. This here, money?" She held up the check. "It's meaningless if there's no love. Goodbye, Andy." She turned and started walking toward the tiled entry, holding the check, holding her head high.

"Jed didn't come back with you."

She stopped in the entry and took in the massive staircase and ornate ceiling. "No, he's looking for his horses. Did you take them, Andy?"

He didn't answer. The anger she often saw in his expression was there again. "I love my cousin. I'd never do that to him."

She hesitated only a second. "You know what, Andy? I believe you. What about your father. Could he have done it?"

Andy only looked away, and she figured she had her answer. She said nothing else, just kept walking to the door and out into the rain and wind. She pulled the door closed behind her, and understood then, how much everything had changed.

Nineteen

It was dark when Jed pulled down his driveway, the wipers flicking back and forth. Diana was just ahead of him, and he parked beside her. The light flicked on inside her SUV as she stepped out and closed the door, and he stepped out too, into darkness and rain. She just stood there behind her vehicle, the rain pouring down over her, and it soaked Jed too.

"You find the horses?" she said.

He shook his head. "I'll start again in the morning. Could've been chased into the hills, the forest. I'll borrow a horse, saddle up, and head out at first light. You get everything squared away with Bonnie and Andy?"

She was tense. Even in the darkness, he could sense the distance he'd created. "Gave Bonnie the check."

"You have any problems with my cousin?" he said. Maybe that was why he was feeling so uneasy.

She shook her head. "No problems, Jed."

"The only way something can work between two people is honesty," he said.

Her blue eyes reached out to him. "I know that. I haven't lied to you. Is that what this is?" she said. She was not a woman to just lie down and let anyone walk on her. He'd figured that much out.

"No. This is about what I told you earlier, how my uncle got in my head and planted those doubts about you letting the horses out. I was being honest with you, Diana, but what you didn't hear was how angry I was at myself, because deep down, I knew you couldn't do something like that."

She threw her arms around him and pressed a kiss to his lips, and he stumbled a bit, holding her against him. He backed her against her SUV, running his hands over her face, feeling the rain coming down, soaking them, as he tasted her, kissing her. He pulled back. Holding her against him, feeling all her softness, he realized he'd never felt this way about any woman.

"Did you mean it, what you said?" he asked.

She was still touching him, her hands on his shoulders. He wanted to get out of the rain, but he didn't want to move. "You're going to have to be more specific. I think I said a lot of things, but I mean what I say."

"You said you loved me. Did you mean that?"

She let her head fall back, the rain coming down in buckets, then looked back to him, and her smile, he swore, could have lit up the world. "Every word. I love you, Jed."

He let his hands linger on her, sliding down over her, then squinted as he looked up into the rain, then back to the redhead who had nearly run him down and turned his life upside down. "How about we get out of the rain?"

"Yeah," she said.

He leaned in again and kissed her, then scooped her up in his arms, and she laughed as he strode through puddles to the crate at the door. Diana reached out and turned the knob to open it, and he set her down inside the small, cramped house, then flicked on the light and closed the door. Thunder boomed, and he saw how soaked she was as she shrugged out of her coat. Her white blouse showed the most perfect breasts he'd ever seen.

He dumped his slicker over the side chair by the door and set his hat overtop of it, and Diana stepped out of her shoes and took a step back. She reached for the elastic holding her soaked red hair back, and Jed pulled off one cowboy boot and then the other, then worked the buttons of his shirt. Diana took a step back down the hall as if she knew where she was going, unbuttoning her blouse with each step back.

"The bedroom on the end," he said. "You're almost there."

She opened her blouse, which was dripping, and dumped it on the floor, just as he did with his shirt. He unfastened his belt and unzipped his jeans as she stepped into the darkened bedroom, with only the faint light from the hall coming in. She tossed her bra to the side and slid down her pants, which appeared stuck, they were so wet, so she sat down at the edge of his small double bed and eased them off. He stepped out of his wet jeans, too, and tossed aside his socks and underwear.

He allowed himself a minute to take in how beautiful she was. As he moved over her, she slid her hands over him, his cheeks. Her thumb was on his lip, and he leaned down and kissed her, tasting her, touching her, loving her. He slid inside her, feeling her breath with his, the rise and fall of her chest, the way her hands slid over his back, pulling him closer to her. This woman was the person he'd been looking for his entire life.

As he lay in her arms, feeling the beat of her heart, the touch of her hand down his back, and the part of him that was now part of her, he felt himself drifting off, and he heard her whisper, "I love you, Jed Friessen, more than you'll ever know."

CHAPTER
Twenty

There was a pounding sound. Diana jumped, blinking for a moment, unsure of where she was, feeling the warmth beside her. A warm hand slid over her where she was pressed against Jed, skin to skin. His hand ran over the flat of her stomach as he pulled away. She realized it was the door, and as she rolled over, Jed was sitting at the edge of the bed. He flicked on the bedside light, illuminating the small boxlike bedroom, with its dresser, three stacked boxes in the corner, and a window with a lace curtain. Jed pulled on a pair of jeans over the most amazing ass she'd ever seen. Diana reached for the quilt, which had been kicked down, and pulled it up over her, feeling the chill.

Jed turned back to her and leaned down to press a kiss to her lips. "Stay here," was all he said, and as she sat up, there was more pounding. "Okay, I'm coming!" he shouted. He stepped into the hall, bare chested, and she heard the door being yanked open, then voices: Jed's and another male voice, one she'd never forget.

"Why are you here, Andy?" Jed was saying.

Diana leaned her head back against the wall, then scooted to the edge of the bed, taking in her wet clothes on the floor along with Jed's. She reached for her linen slacks, which were soaked. Not a chance she was pulling them on, so she strode over to the small dresser and opened a drawer to find a t-shirt. Holding it up, she saw how big it was, but she nonetheless pulled it over her head, feeling the tangles in her damp hair as she lifted it out. The t-shirt draped to mid-thigh.

Diana stepped out of the bedroom and around the corner to the small, boxy living room. The front door was wide open, and it wasn't Jed who saw her first but Andy, standing in the open doorway, wearing a dark slicker. His glance could have set her on fire. Jed seemed to instinctually know she was there, as he was looking right at her now. She took a step closer, right over to him, behind him, resting her hand on his bare arm, feeling the strength he exuded.

"You said you weren't sleeping with my cousin," Andy said. Why did he care so much?

"Not that my life is any of your business, Andy, but if you'll recall, I never answered you," she said.

She thought he swore under his breath. Jed shot her a look, one that asked what was going on. She didn't pull her hand away, and Jed didn't move, as if he would always stand between her and anything that tried to hurt her.

"What the hell, Andy?" he said. "Diana is not your concern; she's mine. In case I didn't make my position clear, you don't talk to her, you don't bully her, and you stay away from her." He sounded rather calm, but touching him, she could feel the tension. He glanced back to her again, letting his gaze linger on the shirt of his she was wearing.

She shrugged. "My clothes are soaked."

He only grunted, and she thought there was amusement there. He turned back to Andy and said, "Now, why are you here?"

Andy let his gaze linger another second on Diana before he dragged it to Jed and inclined his head. "It's about your horses," he said. He didn't look at Diana again, and the way he took in his cousin, she realized he cared more than he'd ever admit. Did Andy really believe she'd hurt Jed?

"What about them?" Jed said. "You know something."

Andy shook his head. "I suspected. You said there were tracks, men's, led out on horseback. You know I would never do that to you." He reached for the switch to flick on the outside light. The rain was still coming down, and Diana realized a horse trailer was hitched behind Andy's truck. "I found them, or rather, I had a feeling. I spoke with a few of the cowboys who handle everything for us without question. Three of them, to be exact. They wouldn't point the finger at Dad, but they told me two of them rode in here last night. They didn't just let your horses out; they had a trailer parked a mile away and loaded them up to take them to the feed lot. They were scheduled to be sold for slaughter on Monday."

Jed leaned down and reached for his cowboy boots on the floor. He shoved his bare feet in and grabbed the slicker he'd tossed over the back of the chair, then shoved it on and pushed past Andy. Diana heard his boots splashing through the puddles.

"It was Todd, wasn't it?" she said. She pulled her arms over her chest, feeling the vulnerability of standing there in just Jed's t-shirt.

Andy was now standing to the side, about to follow Jed. He glanced back to Diana. "I asked my father. He said it wasn't him."

"And you really believe that? Come on, Andy. Your father may not have come right out and said it, but he threatened Jed, this place, his very livelihood—because of me. Because Jed wouldn't toss me out and send me packing." She heard the squeak of the horse trailer. In the light from the barn, Jed was leading his two horses out. She didn't know what to make of Andy, the way he shook his head and looked out into the dark of night before dragging his gaze back to her.

"I don't know what to think," he said. "The cowboys who did it answer to my father. Jed has the horses back, and regardless, if Todd was behind it, no one will speak up. He won't do it again, though."

"You don't know that. Your father is a monster." Diana took in the coats on the hook at the front door. She reached for one of Jed's, a long raincoat, and shrugged it on, then slipped her feet into her flats.

"I know very well what my father is," Andy said, "but let's be clear, Diana, that your mother—"

"Stop it!" she yelled, cutting him off. "I know exactly what she is, or was, but the difference between me and you is she's not in my life now. Look at you, Andy. You say you love Jed, but you're still making excuses for your father, cleaning up after him."

He said nothing, just stepped out of the house, and Diana followed, pulling the door closed behind her. The rain fell on and around them.

"You really care for him?" Andy said.

Diana looked up to him, to the water dripping from his black cowboy hat. "Yeah, I really love him."

Andy said nothing else. He kept walking to the horse trailer and closed up the back, then walked around to his pickup and climbed in. And as Diana strode in the pouring rain to the barn, listening to Andy drive away, she heard Jed murmuring to Scarlett in a stall as he brushed her down. He tossed in a flake of hay before stepping out, securing the stall, and standing beside Diana.

"Andy gone?"

She nodded and slid her hand up his arm, touching him, seeing the love he had for his horses. "Are they okay?"

He looked at her with those whiskey-brown eyes, which touched a part of her she'd never allowed anyone in, a piece she'd closed off to everyone. "Seem to be. You know I love you?"

She felt the smile inside before it touched her lips, and she leaned against Jed as his arm went instinctively around her. He pressed a kiss to the top of her head, and as she looked up to him, he kissed her lips, letting it linger, so tender, filled with so much love.

"This is all I have, Diana," he said. "It isn't much."

She shook her head. "Jed, all I need is you, nothing else."

He didn't look away, and she swore he could see right into her soul. "Marry me."

It took her a second to understand what he'd said. "You're asking me to marry you?"

There it was, that smile. He went down on one knee in the barn, holding her hand with his rough large one, his face in need of a shave and his hair a tangled mess. "Diana Fulton, will you marry me, have children with me, and share your life with me?"

She felt her eyes burn, and Jed blurred for a moment in front of her. She forced a smile to her lips and pulled a breath from the deep ache that burned her chest. She hadn't expected this emotion. "You're damn right I will," she said. "Yes, I will marry you, share every moment with you, and have children with you. I will love you."

He stood and lifted her in his arms, laughing, and then he leaned in as she slid her arms around his shoulders and kissed her again, deeply.

CHAPTER
Twenty~One

Her memories of the day before lingered, as did the memory of her little sister. Diana realized she would always keep Louisa in her heart.

She smoothed down the lace wedding dress she'd bought in town, hearing the laughter outside from Jed's family. His father, Rodney, was tall and distinguished. With his gray hair and his features, he unfortunately resembled Todd, but that was the only similarity. His mother, Becky, was a short woman with warm brown eyes. Diana could see the love that flowed between them and pulled everyone around them into it. His eldest brother, Brad, was another handsome man, with his wife, Emily, and their three children. Jed's second older brother, Neil, was single, devastatingly handsome, and owned a ranch with their father in the Yucatan Peninsula.

The love that flowed in this family for Jed, and for her, was something so wonderful that at times the joy was almost overwhelming. They'd fight for each other.

She had never thought it was possible to love and be loved so deeply.

A slender hand slid over her shoulder and pulled her from her thoughts. "You're stunning, Diana." It was Emily, her brown hair pulled back, wearing a lovely pink chiffon dress with soft folds down the back. She was kind and welcoming, and Diana had asked her to stand up for her. "I know there's a groom out there who's becoming impatient and being teased by his brothers that you've come to your senses and run off."

"I wouldn't do that," she said. "I'm terrified, Emily, because I love him so much."

The smile Emily had was gentle, kind. "Oh, I know that love. I have it with Brad. My advice? Grab it with both hands and hold on. That man loves you. You want to keep him waiting? How about you let him get a look at you walking toward him, say I do, and officially become mister and missus?"

Diana reached for the bouquet Emily held out to her, knowing she didn't want to wait another second more. "Let's do this," she said.

Emily walked to the closed bedroom door and pulled it open, and the two started out down the small hall. She spotted Rodney at the front door in a black tux, his eyes shining with such love and kindness for her.

"Diana, I just want to say how happy Becky and I are that you're going to be part of our family, and how happy you make our son," he said. "We're so proud to be gaining another beautiful, lovely daughter-in-law. I know you don't have family here, Diana, but I'm wondering if you'll allow me the honor of escorting you down the aisle to my son?"

Her heart was so full of emotion, and she turned to

Emily, who nodded to her with a soft smile and so much support. "I would like that," Diana said.

She stepped out of the house, onto the wide board that had taken the place of the crate, and took Rodney's hand, then accepted his arm. He was a kind man who loved his family, the picture of honor and goodness that she'd imagined at one time. She heard the murmur of voices as she was escorted by Rodney into Jed's simple yard, which had been transformed overnight with flowers and chairs and carpeting.

Jed was standing with the minister who presided over them, a graying, portly man dressed in a white shirt and collar and a black coat, as all ministers did. Everyone was standing, and she was aware that Todd and Andy had not been invited.

She handed her bouquet to Emily and took Jed's hands, then spoke her vows and listened to his, and they each slid a simple gold band on the other's finger. Then the minister said, "By the powers vested in me, Jed and Diana, I pronounce you husband and wife."

There was cheering, and then the minister leaned in and said, "You should kiss the bride."

Jed smiled down at her, and she waited as he leaned in and pressed his lips to hers, then kissed her.

The Search

*"Never marry the one you can live with, marry
the one you cannot live without."*

Andy stared at the newspaper image, the hometown article that had been in the lifestyle section. He still didn't know who had left it on his desk so many months ago. One of the maids or property staff, maybe. It hadn't faded yet. The wedding photo of his cousin and Diana was an intimate gut-punch. He'd never expected to receive an invite, but Jed was still his cousin, and he was now married to a woman who was so damn beautiful. Andy had wanted to believe Diana was just like her mother, a woman who'd done anything and everything to get what she wanted. He wondered whether that was why he'd treated her so badly, and now she was untouchable.

"Andy, are you listening to me?" said Pete Jarvis, a short man, round in the middle, balding. He stood in front of Andy's desk, his faded baseball cap in his hands.

Andy shoved the newspaper article and photo back in the top drawer of his desk and closed it. "Do I really want to hear this?" He let out a heavy sigh. Pete was watchful, worried, filled with controlled fury—all because of Andy's father. "So what has he gone and done now?" Andy said without bothering to get up from his leather chair in the library.

Pete worked that damn hat and cleared his throat roughly before responding. "Your father has been seeing Jodie, my sister. Andy, we've known each other a long time. I'm grateful for the job you gave me, overseeing the maintenance on your family's properties, and you know I work hard for you. But I don't want Jodie driven from town when Todd Friessen decides he's done with her."

Andy realized Pete's hand was shaking as he squeezed the brim of his hat until it bent. Andy pulled his hand roughly over his face, hearing the scrape of whiskers, knowing he'd need to shave before dinner. Why could his father still not keep his pants zipped? He scowled and let his gaze linger on Pete before sliding his chair back and striding to the large mahogany-trimmed window. He unbuttoned the cuffs of his black shirt and rolled up the sleeves. Spring was well under way, and the gardeners and landscapers were busy mowing, raking, trimming, and pruning—preparing the gardens scattered over the large estate to bloom in a splendor of colors.

"Jodie's the older one?" Andy didn't turn around. He was trying to remember where Pete lived in town and how big his family was, how many sisters he had. He'd always liked Pete in school; the boy had been a geek, a mechanical genius who could fix anything with his hands, things the average person would just toss out. He came from a large local family with, Andy remembered, five or six kids. He knew Pete was the only boy.

"Terri is the eldest, married last year. Jodie is second, just a year older than me."

Andy glanced over his shoulder to Pete, hearing the edge in his voice. For the life of him, he couldn't remember what Jodie looked like or whether he'd ever met her. Hearing the girl's age, he didn't have a clue what to say.

"Are your mom and dad still living, Pete?" he said. He was trying to remember who Pete's parents were, not that it mattered, but he desperately wanted to put the pieces together and figure out why Todd was focused on a woman as young as Jodie.

"Yes, Andy, they are. Dad's planning on retiring from trucking this year. Mom's part of the local garden club, and this would really hurt her. They don't know, and I only found out at my Friday night poker game, hearing my sister's name tossed out in laughter. It seems everyone around here knew except me."

"I didn't know, so I wouldn't say everyone."

Pete glanced away, but Andy could see the anger simmering. The man firmed his lips as if struggling to remain civil. "Then hear me on this, Andy. My parents don't know about Jodie and your father, but if my dad ever found out, he'd be out here, paying your father a visit. He'd show up with his shotgun, and you and I both know he'd find himself locked up because your father has the sheriff's ear. My family is principled. Right is right, and wrong is wrong. Your father is twice Jodie's age, and he's married—not that it means anything to him, from how he's carried on as long as I can remember. But he's treading on my family now, with his reputation. You and I both know no one has stood up to your father and walked away. How many of the women he's played around with still live in this county? Other than the Claremont girl who stood up to you and your father and married your cousin." Pete was sounding a little more confident.

"Diana," Andy grunted. He stared out the window to a teenager in the yard who had stumbled and tipped over a wheelbarrow of dirt on the green grass.

"Who?" Pete cleared his throat again.

He turned to see Pete staring at him, confused. "Diana was her name, and she was a Fulton, not a Claremont, when she married my cousin. Facts matter. She was never involved with my father."

Tension pulled across his shoulders. He didn't know why it bothered him that people still talked about Diana as if she were worthless. Maybe because he admired her, the way she'd stood up to him, to his father. He'd been wrong about her; she wasn't her mother's daughter. And the fact was that she was now pregnant with his cousin's baby.

"Oh," was all Pete said before gripping that stupid orange baseball cap and bending the brim back again. "Sorry, I forgot. Nice enough girl. And the way she stood up to you, well, the townsfolk admire her for what she has and how she made something of herself, becoming a lawyer and all. Heard they're expecting their firstborn anytime now…"

"What is it you want, Pete?" Andy turned away from the window, feeling the bite in his words. He was so done with talking about Diana, who belonged to his cousin. Maybe that was another reason why he'd been so unsettled lately.

"I want you to talk to your dad and get him to stay away from my sister."

"Why?" Andy walked over to his desk and sat on the edge, gesturing toward Pete. "Get your sister to stay away from my dad. That seems like a simpler solution, don't you think?"

"Well, I tried. But she's starry eyed and love struck, and she seems to think your father is going to leave your mother and marry her." Pete was now getting loud.

There was a clatter as if something had shattered in the hall outside the library, and Andy was already on his feet in his heavy boots, striding across the deep red carpet. A young blonde, her hair tied back in a tight bun, wearing a black maid's dress, was on her knees, picking up pieces of what looked like a shattered vase. Her eyes were a shade of green he'd never seen before, and a feather duster was on the floor beside her. Her face paled.

"I'm so sorry, sir," she said. "The vase slipped. I'll replace it. Please, I need this job…"

What was it about women that they either cowered under him or jumped into his lap? Diana never would have cowered like this. Damn, why couldn't he get her from his mind? He knew Pete was standing there behind him. He wondered how old the maid was. She was picking pieces up with her bare hands, and he thought he saw her hand tremble.

"Don't worry about it," he said. "I'm sure it won't be missed. Just clean it up."

She was slim, likely fresh out of high school. She flicked her gaze to him and nodded, then used her white skirt apron for the bigger pieces. She grabbed a chunk and hissed, and blood dripped onto the floor, but instead of dropping the pieces like a sane person would, she stuffed them into her apron and folded it over, then rose to stand in front of him. She was likely only five foot two, and there was not much to her.

"Again, I'm so sorry, sir. I'll clean this up." She fisted her hand, which was bleeding.

"Jules!" Andy shouted for the head housekeeper, taking in the wide eyes staring up at him. The ridiculous maid's uniform was about as appealing as a grain sack, starched and buttoned right to her throat. "You're bleeding. Give me your hand. Stop worrying about the damn floor. Pete, grab that garbage can by my desk."

Her hand trembled as she slowly held it out, the other gripping the apron holding the pieces of the broken vase. The cut was deep and oozing blood. Andy heard the footsteps of Jules, a plump, graying woman, and then Pete was there with the garbage can.

"Yes, Mr. Friessen?" Jules said. Her eyes widened before she frowned, wringing her hands, looking down at the startled girl. "My God, Laura, what have you done now? That was Mrs. Friessen's Chinese vase! It's worth more than you make in a year," she snapped harshly. "I'm so sorry, Mr. Friessen. I'll see that she's gone by the end of the day."

The blonde froze, her hand stiffening and her face burning crimson. So her name was Laura.

Andy took the garbage can from Pete, who said nothing, and held it out to the young maid for the broken pieces she still clutched in her apron. "Let go," was all he said, and after she had dumped the pieces in, he handed the garbage can back to a silent Pete. Jules was still there, too, with her ever-present frown, and Andy said, "Take off your apron, Jules."

Her eyes were an average shade of blue, and the way she stared at him, he knew she didn't understand.

"I need your apron, Jules."

She shook her head, then scrambled to untie her white apron, her double chin wobbling. Andy took it from her before she could add another word, and he reached for Laura's hand, which was still bleeding, and wrapped the apron around it. He was stuck on what Jules had said about firing the young girl because she'd broken a damn vase. This entire thing with his dad, his family, was getting out of hand.

"Jules, you're not firing anyone today," he said. "Get real, would you? It was an accident. Look around this house. There's too much crap, glass, useless objects. Honestly, I don't remember even seeing a vase. That's how much it's going to be missed. Laura, is it?"

The scared blonde lifted those wide green eyes up to him. He could feel how tense she was from how stiffly she stood. "Yes, sir, Laura's my name," she said, then swallowed.

He knew when someone was scared. Blood was soaking through the apron. "That cut is deep," he said. "Jules, you need to take her to get it stitched up. I can clean the rest up myself. I'm sure there's a broom around here someplace."

Three pairs of eyes stared at him as though he'd sprouted a second head.

"I know how to use a broom," he said. "You think I haven't cleaned up my share of broken glass before? I can tell you, growing up, it was easiest for me to clean up everything I broke, crystal, ornaments, glasses, plates, and toss it out before any of you knew."

Jules frowned. He'd learned the hard way that his mother cared more for her things than for her son. When he was five, running through the house, he'd knocked over a side table and broken a crystal decanter, and his mother, the ice queen, had shooed him off to be raised by the housekeeper. Now everyone was making a big deal over a vase he couldn't even remember.

"Stop standing around, Jules," he said. "Laura, go and get that cut taken care of." He knew it had come out sharply, as Jules and Laura left immediately. He let out a heavy sigh, staring at the small pieces of glass on the floor beside a few drops of blood. Pete was still holding the damn garbage, so Andy reached for it and said, "Are we done, Pete?"

Pete stood there, holding his hat, determined, showing a backbone Andy didn't see often. "Andy, my sister?"

"I'll handle it," he said. How, he didn't have a clue. "And no, she won't be run from town."

Pete put his hat back on and, evidently satisfied, strode to the front door. As he pulled it open and left, Andy headed down the hall to the kitchen, to the closet where he remembered all the brooms, mops, and cleaners were stored. He pushed open the door and took in the empty, quiet kitchen, different than it had been in his childhood, now with white cupboards, a green slate floor, and black appliances. The corner closet he remembered had a glass door and was now a walk-in pantry.

"What the hell?" he said as he glanced around, wondering when it had all changed. He was headed for a tall cupboard on the opposite side, close to the back door the staff used, when he heard the phone ring. It was a cordless phone, one of many in a house that size, and because he was right there, he reached for it. "Andy here." He looked around behind him, still distracted.

The closet he'd opened held coats and shelves of uniforms and aprons.

"Andy, it's Diana."

A voice he'd never expected to hear, not calling him.

"Diana…how are you?"

What was he supposed to say to his cousin's wife? She was the reason he figured there'd now always be a rift between him and Jed.

"I'm worried about Jed," she said. "He took that new stallion out and was supposed to be back before lunch. I've called his cell phone and left about a dozen messages. He doesn't answer, and now it says his mailbox is full."

He turned around in the empty kitchen and took in the digital clock on the stove, seeing it was 6:40 p.m. "Jed's one of the best riders out there. Maybe he—"

"I knew it was a mistake, calling." She cut him off rather sharply. "But I didn't know who else to call. I don't know the forest, all the places he rides off to, or where to start looking. I shouldn't have called, Andy. I'll go look myself."

"Diana, wait, what do you think you're going to do? Aren't you pregnant and due anytime?" He put his hand to his face, pulling it over it again, wondering what Jed was thinking sometimes.

"My husband is missing. Being pregnant isn't going to keep me from looking for him. This isn't like Jed. He always comes back when he says. I know something is wrong."

Andy heard the worry in her voice and knew she was right; Jed was as steady as they came and then some. "Just stay put," he said. "It'll take me about twenty minutes, but I'm on my way."

He heard her soft breath on the other end. "Thank you," was all she said before she hung up.

Andy set the phone back in the holder. The last time he'd seen Diana and Jed had been the night he'd brought Jed's horses back. The cowboys who'd taken them still worked there, and his father had said only one thing when he'd confronted him: "The boy needs to know his place and who his family is."

But to Andy, Jed was family, and right now, he was missing. The months that had passed, and Andy realized his lingering anger was something he could no longer live with. He walked to the back door and pulled it open to see his pickup and trailer parked beside the fifty-stall barn. In less than five minutes, he had hitched the trailer to his pickup, loaded up his mare, Ladystar, and was pulling out onto the highway, taking in the thick clouds overhead, bearing what looked like another night of heavy rain.

Twenty~Three

Diana was leading a dark mare from the barn when Andy pulled in. As he stepped out of his pickup and into one of many puddles, he took in the small, rundown house. Diana's brilliant red hair was pulled back, shimmering under the setting sun. Her eyes had always been the killer for him; the deep blue touched something inside him that made it damn difficult to breathe as he took in the sight of her. She wore blue jeans and a long pink shirt with a soft blue sweater pulled overtop, her belly large, carrying his cousin's child. She appeared ready to deliver any day.

He was startled to realize that, although she was pregnant, she was still the sexiest woman ever, a sight to behold. He still wished she were his, even that the baby she carried were his. Hell, he wished for a lot of things. Maybe it was her strength that bothered him more than anything.

"Andy, thanks for coming." Diana tied the mare to a rail outside the barn.

"Well, of course I've come. What happened, Diana? You said he took a horse out?"

The wind picked up and blew strands of her red hair over her eyes, and she brushed it back, the simple gold band flashing on her finger. She pulled in a heavy breath, and he wondered if it was because she was so pregnant that worry sat heavy around her. He felt it just standing there, looking down at her and the horse she rested her hand on, taking in the disarray of the place. The barn door needed to be repaired, and a tarp was covering the roof. What looked like endless repairs were needed everywhere.

"He said he would be back for lunch," Diana said again. "He's training that stallion, Red, that he bought before Christmas at auction. It was a good deal he got him for, and he's training him every day so he can take him on pack trips he's scheduled this summer. He's been taking him out longer and longer, but he has a cell phone with him. I made him get one because he knows I worry, but he's not answering. Sometimes he goes out of range, but not for long, and he wouldn't do that now, with the baby's due date so close. It's after seven, so he's seven hours late. You know Jed; he doesn't do that, not ever."

Diana pulled the sweater closer, and he thought she must be cold. He didn't think before shrugging out of his lined denim jacket and draping it over her shoulders. She stiffened when he touched her and flicked up that gaze. She appeared tired, with dark circles under her eyes.

"Diana, you look so tired," he said. "Is Jed treating you okay?"

Her eyes flashed with a fire he remembered, and she

stepped back, slipped his coat off as if she'd thought better of it, and held it out to him. "Jed treats me just fine. He respects me, and he loves me. I'm just tired all the time now. It's called being pregnant. Andy, please take your coat."

He could see her determination. She was such a strong woman, and there was something about her. He wished he'd never done what he'd done. Damn, his cousin was a lucky man. "Well, maybe Jed shouldn't be leaving you alone right now. Look at you, seriously, out here alone." Even he could hear how unreasonable he sounded.

"I'm pregnant, Andy, not an invalid," Diana said. "I told Jed the same thing. Life goes on. He's got a horse to train, and we have bills to pay. Now, if it's all the same to you, could you help me saddle Scarlett so we can start looking before it's fully dark?"

It was in that second he realized what she was saying. He took in the horse and then Diana's very pregnant belly. "You're not going anywhere," he said. "You're not getting on a horse, as pregnant as you are. I'll go find Jed. You stay here." Andy was already walking to his trailer and unlatching the door. He led Ladystar out and walked her to another post by Scarlett. Meanwhile, Diana had tossed a saddle blanket on Scarlett and strode back inside the barn.

"Diana what are you doing?" he called out. "I said you're not going. I'll look for Jed. Look at you; you can barely walk. Go into the house and wait. Put your feet up."

She never even tossed him a glance as she pulled on a large gray slicker over her sweater and reached for the saddle.

"Stop!" he shouted. In two steps, he was there, his hands on the saddle, taking it before she could lift it off the pegs it sat on. "Diana, no fucking games here. Stop. You're not coming."

Her mouth was tight, and she flicked those tired blue eyes up to him. "Well, actually, yes, I am. I can still ride. I know my limits, Andy, and Scarlett is gentle. She doesn't spook. I won't be bullied by you. I just need to be careful. I'm not going to stand here, arguing with you, while my husband is out there. Something's happened. He could be hurt or worse…" Her voice caught, and when she glanced away, he could see she was determined not to cry, but a tear slipped out, and she swiped it away roughly as if angry at herself for letting it fall.

"Diana, you're risking Jed's baby by getting on that horse," he said. "I can move a lot faster without you."

She was already shaking her head. "Then you can leave me and ride ahead, but I'm going."

He started to the mare and tossed the saddle over her, flicking his gaze back to Diana. "Jed is going to kill me," he said under his breath, but he knew Diana was right: Time was ticking, and Jed was seven hours late. Diana strode over, her hand resting on her swollen belly. She wiped her hair from her face again in the wind.

"You listen to me, Diana," he said. "You ride behind me, and you ride where I tell you and nowhere else. You're going to take it slow and steady." He shook his head as he took in his cousin's wife, a woman he realized would walk right into hell for her husband. She was the kind of woman he wished were his. He finished saddling Scarlett and took the reins Diana held out to him.

"Thank you, Andy."

"Yeah, well, don't thank me just yet. You're Jed's

wife, not mine, and I know my cousin well enough to know that when he sees you on a horse, looking the way you do, he won't be happy."

If she were his, Andy thought, he'd never let her anywhere near a horse or out of his bed until the baby was born. But he couldn't say that.

He watched Diana reach for a wide-brimmed hat from the hook and put it on, then walk over to the horse he'd saddled and lift her foot into the stirrup. As he put his hand on her, touching her, helping her up into the saddle, he realized there was so much depth to this woman, including a stubborn streak a mile wide. Once she set her mind to something, nothing and no one could change it. Damn, his cousin really was a lucky man.

Twenty~Four

"Are you sure he came this way?" Andy called back, guiding Ladystar up a narrow trail with heavy brush on both sides. He had lost Jed's trail when they hit the beaver dam, and getting through had been worse than he'd expected. They were in a thick patch of mud, the water too high for his comfort. Andy had yelled more than once at Diana because the way they were going was becoming too dangerous for her.

He already knew that if something happened to Diana, going to hell would be the lightest sentence he received.

"Jed said he was taking him through the beaver dam today," she said. "I've been through here with Jed only a few times. I've never had to worry about him on a horse."

The sun was already setting, and being out there in the dark wasn't ideal. Andy, too, had never had to worry about someone before like he was worrying about

Diana. She didn't know that unpredictable things happened all the time with horses.

"How are you holding up?" He knew he'd asked half a dozen times already.

"I'm fine. Stop worrying about me."

"You may as well just say, 'Stop breathing,' because worrying about you is the one thing I won't stop doing. You're Jed's very pregnant wife, and if you fell off the horse, Diana—"

"Stop it, Andy. I don't want that in my head. Can you see any tracks? Keep looking. Where is he?"

He shook his head. It was getting harder in the waning light to see the tracks. He was good on a horse, damn good, but tracking was something Jed had a sixth sense for, not him. He reached into his saddlebag, which held an emergency first aid kit and a flashlight. He took the latter out and flicked it on at the ground, leading his horse through heavy bushes.

"I think Jed went through here," he said and glanced back to see Diana holding the saddle horn and moving in behind him as he pushed through. It was a logging road covered in gravel and dirt. He thought he'd heard something. A bear, wolf, cougar? Those were the last things he wanted there with Diana.

"Diana, tighten up on those reins!" He knew it had come out rather sharply.

Then he spotted a horse just through the bushes, saddled and grazing. That had to be the stallion.

"That's Red!" Diana called out. "Andy, that's Jed's horse."

If he'd ever had illusions that Diana didn't love Jed, they'd been dispelled. He slowly approached the stallion, taking in the size of it. Red jerked his head back after taking in a mouthful of brush.

"Whoa, easy, boy," Andy said, then tucked his flashlight back in his saddlebag. He lifted a hand to the horse, who was skittish and wild eyed, as he got down from Ladystar. "Easy there. Diana, take Ladystar's reins."

He held his horse's reins out to her, knowing Red was two seconds from bolting. And where the hell was Jed? She took the reins, and for just a moment, he took in everything about her—the way she was seated in the saddle, her hair pulled back, with strands blowing everywhere from under that wide-brimmed hat, the emotion in her eyes, a face that had no hint of makeup, right down to her clothes, more for comfort than anything else. Damn, she was the most beautiful sight.

"If she pulls or bolts, let her go," he said, then made his way easy and slowly over to Red. "Easy there, boy," he said, then reached for the reins, but only one dangled. The other had been ripped right off. The horse squealed, a sound that went right through Andy. It was unsettling, dealing with a horse this unpredictable. His eyes were wild, and he backed up and pulled on the rein, skittish. "Easy, boy, I'm not going to hurt you," Andy murmured softly to the frightened horse, who neighed again. *A stallion, seriously, Jed? What the hell are you thinking?*

"Andy, where is Jed?" Diana called out.

Andy listened to the sounds of the forest, hearing nothing. "Jed!" he shouted, and the horse squealed again, his energy through the roof. "Whoa, easy, boy." Andy carefully reached into his pocket and pulled out his cell phone. "Diana, what's Jed's number?"

Red was pulling at Andy again. The horse was becoming the kind of problem he couldn't have around

Diana. Damn, he wished she were at home, waiting, where she should be.

She rattled off Jed's number to him, and he dialed it, but it didn't ring, just went to voicemail, and the automated system said, "This mailbox is full." He hung up and shoved his phone back in his pocket, shaking his head, seeing the worry staring down at him. "Right to voicemail, didn't even ring, which doesn't help us hear him. How many messages did you leave? His mailbox is full."

Diana shut her eyes for a second, and he knew she understood what he was saying. She was a smart woman, perceptive. He didn't have to explain. "Andy, what if Jed's lying hurt somewhere?" she said. "It's almost dark. We've got to find him."

The stallion tried to rear up, mud half up his legs. Red was young and spirited—and spooked. Andy could feel him trembling, heart pounding so hard that he might bolt at any moment. Then he saw it, a gash on the side of the horse, with dried blood.

"Andy, we have to keep looking!"

It was getting dark, and Diana was fast becoming an outline beside him. He reached for the reins to Ladystar, who appeared uncertain because of the stallion.

"We do, but not with you, Diana," he said. "We need to head back and get a search party out here, start at first light."

Ladystar danced a bit and bumped Scarlett, and Diana grabbed the saddle horn.

"Whoa, easy, girl," he started. He reached up and yanked the bridle from Red, then said, "Go," and the stallion took off the other way.

"Andy, that's Jed's horse! What are you doing?"

He climbed back into the saddle on Ladystar. "He'll be fine out here, but you won't be. I can come back out and look after we get help to find Jed."

She was shaking her head. "We came this far, Andy. I'm not going back. We have to keep looking. How far could he be from here and where we found Red?" She squinted into the darkness, and it sounded as if she were short of breath.

He considered how much to say. "You're a big girl, Diana. The truth of the matter is Red could have run a long ways. He's got a gash in him, and his legs are covered in mud. Horses can cover a long distance in a short time."

She turned her head, still looking into the darkness. "We're wasting time, Andy," was all she said before she lifted the reins and urged Scarlett into a walk. "I know there's a meadow not far from here off the logging road that Jed talks about. It's a spot he takes his groups on horseback. There's a lake up there, a great spot to camp."

Andy knew this area well, even the spots Jed would ride and take his groups out, the beginners and those who were in it for the challenge. But the spring temperatures were still dropping close to freezing as soon as the sun went down. His breath fogged. He nodded. "Stay behind me, Diana. Where my horse goes, you go. Watch my horse's hoofs. She's shoed, so if she goes over any rocks, there will be sparks."

They reached the top of the logging road and angled right down the narrow trail. The dark had never bothered him, but it was different tonight. Everything about this could go wrong. Diana's horse skittered and neighed, and Andy kicked Ladystar and turned her, reaching for Scarlett's reins.

"Dammit!" he said. "I knew this was a bad idea. You're barely sitting up, so don't push it, Diana, because if I decide to turn us around and head back, there'll be little you can do about it. No, we can't stay out here all night. You're going to get hurt. I'm taking you back," he yelled.

Then he thought he heard something.

"Andy, did you hear that? Shh, listen."

He was holding the reins now and turned his head. "Jed!" he shouted, then heard it again off to the right.

"Over here!"

Sweet Jesus! That was Jed.

"Jed!" Diana shouted. "Andy, that's Jed!"

"Jed, keep shouting so I can find you," he yelled, dragging Diana's horse behind him and not letting her have the reins.

"Over here!"

He was so close, and there was no mistaking Jed's voice, but he sounded off. Andy juggled both reins in one hand and flicked on the flashlight with the other. There he was, against a tree, maybe thirty feet ahead, wearing just a long-sleeved shirt and sitting awkwardly. He wasn't sure if it was blood or dirt caked down the side of his face.

"Jed, you're hurt!" Diana screamed, and she struggled to get down.

Andy hopped to the ground and grabbed her, lifting her out of her saddle, and she hurried around Scarlett over to Jed, who wasn't moving. She knelt beside him.

"How bad is it?" she said, her hand on him.

Andy tied both horses to a tree and hurried over to

Jed, who gave him a hard, murderous glare. He approached Jed carefully, the flashlight flickering over him. He squinted in the light, and Andy didn't miss how he was struggling to breathe.

"What the hell is my wife doing out here and on horseback?" he said. "Are you crazy, Diana, getting on a horse right now?" He was having a hard time talking, his breathing rough, and he had a gash on the side of his head.

Andy hunkered down beside him. "You can kill me after we get you out of here," he said. "You're a sight, that's for sure." He needed a second to process the overwhelming relief that they'd found him.

"No one's going to kill anyone, Jed," Diana said rather sharply. "You think I wasn't going to come after you? Noon, Jed! You said you'd be back at noon. Where is your damn cell phone? I called and called…" She had her hand on him and pressed a kiss to the side of his head. "Your head's bleeding." She kissed him again and wiped a tear from her eye.

"It's just a cut," Jed said. "It'll be fine. Hey, babe, it's okay. I couldn't find my phone, sitting here after that damn horse threw me. It probably fell out of my pocket. A black bear and her cubs caught me off guard, and he reared up. Haven't been thrown since I was a kid. You called Andy?"

Seeing Jed and Diana from a distance had felt so different than it felt right now. He saw the love that connected them, and it touched him, leaving him, for a moment, feeling so damn lonely.

"I didn't know who else to call," she said. "A search party would have been next."

Andy shone his flashlight at the gash on Jed's head.

"How hard did you hit your head? It looks deep, made a hell of a mess of your face." He noted how Jed leaned heavily against the tree and the odd angle of his right leg. "Is it broken?" he asked. Two branches lay nearby with long strips of bark peeled from them as if Jed had been trying to fasten a splint. Of course he had, and he'd likely have found a way. Jed was driven by the kind of grit few had.

"Yup, hurts like hell," Jed said roughly.

"Anywhere else?" Andy asked in an unusually calm voice as he rested a hand on Jed's shoulder.

"Yeah, pretty sure I busted a rib."

Andy let out a rough laugh, then pulled the back of his hand over his forehead. "Diana, take the flashlight," he said and held it out to her.

Jed winced when Diana rubbed his shoulder. Then she took the flashlight, and Andy pulled out his cell phone.

"No service," he said, letting his gaze linger on Diana. She only shook her head. Jed appeared more aware of how dire the situation was, but at least they'd found him.

"How are we going to get him out of here with a broken leg?" Diana said.

Andy had thought over the best and worst cases, considering how dark it was, the fact that they had no fire going, and Jed's injuries could be worse than just a busted rid and broken leg. A punctured lung and a head injury were just two possibilities he'd considered.

"Is there water in the saddlebag?" she asked, looking right at him.

Andy nodded. "Yeah, a couple bottles."

She didn't wait, just struggled to her feet and shone the light ahead of her to the horses.

"I wish you wouldn't have brought her," Jed said. "The only thing that gave me some peace was knowing Diana was safe at home. She shouldn't be on a horse, Andy. She's too pregnant."

"You think I didn't try to stop her?" He shook his head. "I did, but she refused and was going to saddle Scarlett herself if I didn't. She'd have followed me and been out here alone. Think about that. She's your wife and damn stubborn. Oh, and we found your horse. What were you thinking with that stallion? I let him go. It was too dangerous, having him around Diana. I can come back out and look for him tomorrow. He'll be fine."

Jed swore under his breath, then patted Andy's arm. "I guess I owe you."

Andy sighed. "Yeah, well, we can discuss who owes who and who's buying the six pack when we get out of here. Hate to say this, but the best thing would be for me to go for help. I can ride faster alone, but I don't want to leave you two out here. If I splint your leg, do you think you can sit in a saddle?"

Jed scowled. Andy knew his cousin would never admit it if he couldn't. The flashlight flickered over him as Diana strode back around, kneeling down beside him again, and Jed's gaze went right to her. "The day I can't sit in a saddle will be the day you're tossing dirt over my grave," he said.

"Don't talk like that." Diana unscrewed the water bottle and held it to his lips. "Come on, drink."

His cousin swallowed some water, then coughed, spitting some out. Diana pulled a rag from the pocket of the slicker she wore, poured water on it, and wiped some of the dried blood from Jed's face. Andy hadn't expected her to be this calm.

"Jed, put this on. It's cold out here." Diana slipped out of the slicker, but Jed was holding his hand up.

"No, Diana, put it back on. I'll be fine. I've been out in worse. You have to stay warm for the baby."

Andy stood up, trying to figure out how he was going to do this. He strode over to Ladystar in the dark, hearing the back and forth between Jed and Diana. The words went past him, but he could feel the love each had for the other. He untied the blanket behind his saddle, pulled out the first aid kit and walked back over to Jed and Diana, kicking at the sticks on the ground, then squatted back down and unzipped it to pull out a roll of elastic tensor bandages and rolled gauze.

"Jed, I am so mad at you," Diana said. "You scared the life out of me. You're not going out alone with that stallion again. You could have been killed, and then what would I do without you? If you die on me, I won't forgive you!"

Andy was beginning to feel like the unwelcome third party as Diana dabbed at the cut on Jed's forehead a little harder than necessary. He winced.

"Ow, Diana, ease up." Jed grabbed her arm, holding her, and again she leaned down, her head against his. Jed took the effort to put his arm around her, knocking her hat off as he leaned in and pressed a kiss to her messy hair.

"Okay, sorry to break this up," Andy said. "Diana, Jed, let's get this over with and get you down to the hospital. Diana, I'm going to need your help." He shook out the blanket, and she was already nodding. "Let's get this around you, Jed, to warm you up."

Diana was on her knees, helping Jed sit forward. He hissed, hurting way more than he'd ever let on, as Andy draped the blanket around his shoulders, then picked up the two sticks. He could see the break even through Jed's jeans. It was bad, just below the knee. Andy didn't need to say anything about how badly it was going to hurt. Beads of sweat covered Jed's forehead, mixed with the dried blood.

Diana was holding the flashlight, and Andy didn't miss the hint of fear in Jed's expression as he said, "You're making this damn painful. Get on with it, for fuck's sake."

Andy tore strips from the gauze and slid them under Jed's leg. "You want a stick to bite down on? Because I'm fresh out of bullets."

"Just get it done, already."

Andy reached around for the two sticks. There was a third as well, but it was too big. He set one on each side over the gauze and glanced to the wide eyes of Diana, which he could just make out in the dimness, as she rested her hands on Jed's shoulders. Damn, she was rattled.

Andy nodded. "Look at me, Jed. You know it's going to hurt, but it will only be a second, and then we're getting out of here," he said, then pulled hard, tying, and didn't stop even as his cousin yelled and tensed, fighting a war to stay still. He tied the last of five knots, better than nothing. Jed appeared drained as he sagged against the tree, close to passing out. "Listen up, Jed. I'm going to get you on Ladystar. Do you want me to tie you on?"

"Hell, no. I can sit just fine. Just get me on her," he bit out, but Andy wasn't so sure.

"Diana, after I get Jed on my horse, I'll get you on yours, and then I'll lead both of you down. It'll be slow, but as soon as we're in cell range, I'll call for help."

She nodded, grateful, holding tight to Jed.

"Jed, put your arm around my shoulder," Andy said and leaned down, then somehow lifted Jed, who was yelling and swearing. The light from the flashlight flickered on the ground in front of him as he half-carried Jed, who hopped on his other foot, over to Ladystar. "Lean on me, but get that other foot in the stirrup." Damn, his cousin was heavy!

"Fuck," Jed said again, then nearly went over the side.

Andy grabbed him, holding him, his splinted leg just dangling. He didn't need any light to see the agony Jed was in. He stepped right up to him, his hand on him, and kept his voice low so Diana couldn't hear. "You hold on to the horn with both hands. Being prideful is one thing; being stupid is another."

Jed only nodded.

Andy tapped his arm. "Let me get Diana seated, and then we're getting out of here. You think you're going to pass out, you let me know."

"Stop talking so much. Let's go, already," Jed bit out as he struggled for breath.

Andy took the flashlight from Diana, who had the wide-brimmed hat on again. "Your turn."

She already had her foot in the stirrup and was pulling herself up. Andy put his hand on her, pushing her up, and then she was seated, reaching for the reins.

"How about if I take both and you hold on?" he said.

She shook her head. "No, I'm fine. I can follow you. You have enough with leading my husband on the horse and getting us out of here."

"Diana…" Jed started.

Andy put his hand on Diana's saddle, beside her leg. "It's dark," he said. "We've got all kinds of things out here, especially cougars, who hunt at night."

"I know, Andy, but you have only two hands, one for the flashlight and one to lead Ladystar. Let's go."

Of all times for him not to have brought a lead rope and halter! That would have made it easier, and he knew how right Diana was.

"You stay right behind," he said. "She spooks, you pull the reins and circle her."

She was nodding. "I know what to do, Andy."

Jed said nothing, and Andy shone the flashlight at the ground. His cousin was leaning over the saddle horn, holding it.

"Ready?" he said. "This won't be comfortable."

Jed only nodded.

"Let's go!" Andy called out loudly, not just for Jed but to scare off anything out in the dark that could hurt or spook the horses and become one more problem he didn't want to deal with.

They were halfway down in the black of night. Andy had stopped more than a few times because the dark, shadowy forest didn't look the same as it did in the light of day. He'd listened to Diana's calming voice, the way she spoke to Jed, who had only grunted for the last little bit. Then he heard Diana hiss.

"You two doing okay back there?" he called out.

"Oh no," Diana said in a low voice.

"Diana, what's wrong?" Jed sounded weak.

In the second that ticked by with Diana saying nothing, Andy flashed his flashlight to her. She was leaning forward, and he thought she was wincing. Instinct had him reaching for her reins, turning Ladystar.

"Diana, what's wrong?" he yelled.

She let out a sharp breath. "I think I'm in labor."

"What?" He wasn't sure if it was Jed or him that had shouted it. He took in the darkness of the forest. There was no way in hell she was delivering a baby way out there. This was definitely now the worst case. Andy held both sets of reins and tucked the flashlight under his arm, then yanked his cell phone from his pocket. Still no cell service.

"How can you be in labor? The baby's not due for another week," Jed called out.

"Diana, can you hang on?" Andy yelled. "I still have no service." He shoved his cell phone back in his pocket. "We've got to move."

She nodded. "Just get going," she bit out, and he could see how uncomfortable she was.

"Come on, girls, let's go," he said to the horses, leading both now and picking up his pace. They were back on the old logging road, and he pulled out his phone again, seeing two bars. The relief that hit in that second had him silently thanking the universe. He dialed emergency and heard the ring.

"Nine one one, what's your emergency?" said the person on the other end, and Andy knew help would soon be on the way.

Twenty-Five

"Are you sure you're supposed to be out of the hospital so soon?" Andy said. He was standing just inside the door, his hands shoved in the pockets of his black slicker as the rain came down outside. He couldn't sit in Jed's cramped living room, with a bassinet in the corner, a baby swing, and piles of baby gifts half the townsfolk had sent.

Jed was on the sofa, his right leg in a walking cast, resting on the scratched table, which looked like something from his barn. He had three stitches on his forehead and a busted rib that, as the doctor had said, he was damn lucky hadn't punctured his lung. He stared down at his newborn son with an expression that was almost magical.

"You think I'm letting Diana come home without me?" he said. "I'm fine. I got that cane to help get around, and Mom's flying out to help until I'm back on my feet. Dad said they're going to camp out in one of the cabins since this place isn't big enough, but not sure how long that will last, as those cabins still don't have heat, and there's not much to them."

Diana wasn't moving that fast, either, but then, Andy couldn't believe they were both home, considering it had been only a few days since he'd seen the flashing lights of the ambulance at the end of the service road. He wondered whether the two of them had any idea how scared he'd been.

"Jed, we're going to need a bigger house for these gifts alone," Diana said. "Will you look at all these clothes? The only way Danny can wear all these is if I change him into a new outfit three times a day." She had her hair pulled back and was still in maternity clothes as she sat down beside Jed on the loveseat. The image of love flowed through them, and awe for the new life. "Andy, do you want some coffee?"

"No," he said. "Thank you, Diana, but I need to get going. I just wanted to stop in and check on you two, try to talk you into coming to stay with me. You know Caroline and Todd are gone right now. Todd's somewhere down in the Caribbean, I think, and Caroline is over at that house she has in the south of France. It's just me rambling around that big old house, and it's lonely. I could use the company, and there's some help until you're both on your feet…" He stopped talking because it sounded so foolish now as he spoke it out.

"Thanks for the offer, Andy, but we're good here." Jed looked up at him, and he wasn't sure what he was thinking. Diana let her gaze linger on her husband, and Andy ached because he'd never thought a woman could love a man like that.

"Diana and I wanted to thank you, Andy, for sending out your stable hands to handle the chores and look after the horses," Jed said. "It's a big weight off me. And I guess I never thanked you for coming up after me, for everything you did."

Diana rested her hand on Jed's arm. "You said you were going to ask him." She nudged Jed and slid her hand over their newborn son, his fingers, his legs. Andy felt so damn uncomfortable, trying to figure out how they would go forward.

"I was getting to that," Jed said, then lifted his gaze to Andy again, revealing the bruising on the side of his head and another scratch on his cheek. "Diana and I wanted to ask if you'd be Danny's godfather."

Andy wasn't sure he'd heard right.

"We also named him Daniel Anderson Friessen," Diana said, lifting her gaze to him. "If it hadn't been for you, Andy, I would hate to think what could have happened."

"You named him after me?" Andy said. "Wow, I don't know what to say. Thank you. I would love to be this little guy's godfather." He didn't know where the tightness in his chest had come from. It spilled through him, and he had to look past Jed and Diana, out the window to the old barn and the tarp that was keeping the rain out. "You two sure you're going to be okay?"

Diana offered him a soft smile, while Jed said, "We're good, Andy. Thanks again for coming after me —and for looking after my wife."

Andy only inclined his head, then pulled open the door and stepped out onto the makeshift step into the rain. He pulled the door closed and took a second to just feel everything of the last two days. Outside the emergency room at the hospital where they'd set Jed's leg, Andy had been told the baby's heartbeat had slowed and the OB on call had rushed Diana in for an emergency C-section. He had walked back and forth from Jed in the emergency room to Diana in the maternity ward, doing everything he could to fix every wrong choice he'd made until then.

Now in the pouring rain, he made his way over to his pickup. Red, the young stallion, was being led into the barn by one of the stable hands he'd sent over, and he knew the vet had been there that morning. It had been the day before that the stallion had found his own way home.

Andy looked back to the simple rundown house, a property that needed so much work, but the love there was bigger than he could have imagined. He slid behind the wheel of his pickup and made his way back toward town. The rain had eased up, and he was thinking of the big, luxurious, empty house he was going back to.

That morning, he'd talked to his father and told him to stay away from Pete's sister, but Todd had only laughed. Andy squeezed the steering wheel, wondering for the first time what his life would be like if he weren't always cleaning up after Todd Friessen. Maybe that was another reason he envied Jed.

As he stopped at the lights in town, he didn't know what made him look over to the grocery store on the corner. There stood the scrawny blond maid who'd broken that ugly vase. She held a plastic bag, her hair hanging long and loose, and she was holding the hand of a small boy. What was her name, Laura? She opened the back door of a beat-up old Volvo with a rusted fender and helped the little boy in. When she glanced his way, he wondered whether she knew it was him. She didn't smile, and she didn't wave. She just leaned in and buckled the child in the back seat, then climbed in the car and drove away.

A car horn honked, rousing Andy, and he realized the light was green. He continued on home, certain of only one thing: For him, something had changed.

Turn the page for a sneak peek of
*THE AWAKENING the next book in THE OUTSIDER
SERIES*
Available in print, eBook and audio

The Awakening

A young woman who's lost everything, and the wealthy rancher who must choose between his family's power and his conscience to help her.

—Such an amazing story! The despair and the kindness from others gave this story a real meaning... Down2earth Girl

—Well written story about overcoming the stigma of "lower" class and "upper" class! It was love story that kept me reading to see if it would turn out the way I hoped! ... Bartow

—"The author brought to life a story that is all but too often right in front of our faces, but we are too busy to see." Amazon Reviewer Grammy

In THE AWAKENING, Laura, a young single mother is barely making ends meet working as a maid at the

Friessen mansion. Until one day she is fired, the
next day she is evicted, and two days later her son is
taken away.

Wealthy rancher Andy Friessen can have any woman he
wants, but when Laura is fired by his mother over something he was responsible for, well his conscience gets the
better of him and he steps in to help. The problem is
when he goes looking for Laura he not only discovers
she's been living in her car, but the state took her child
away.

With Andy standing beside her through a courtroom
fiasco, they must fight together to regain custody of
her son.

The Awakening

CHAPTER 1

"Get this god-awful tree out of here!" Andy shouted as he stormed into the grand library, his dark hide boots barely making a sound on the rich scarlet carpet as he cut a path toward his large mahogany desk. The library was his domain, a showpiece of the Friessen mansion. It was a very masculine room, filled with browns and reds, dark wood, leather chairs, oil paintings worth more than the estate, a room Andy had appointed as his office.

"Sir, your mother ordered this tree and left instructions for it to be set up and decorated in this very room," Laura, a very young, pretty blond maid responded without glancing Andy's way. She pursed her soft red lips and continued to hang bright green ornaments on the vibrant white tree.

Andy slid his large hand under a branch of the Douglas-fir. "I didn't know that fir trees grew white. What, did you have this dyed?"

This time, the maid glanced at Andy with those sea-green eyes, wearing the ugly maid uniform that hung like a grain sack from what he could only imagine was a slim body underneath. It was the most unflattering getup, with a starched collar and buttoned up to her chin. And, of course, Andy being Andy, he couldn't help wondering how she'd look in something low cut, slinky, and black. Preferably something that fit her like a second skin and showed off the generous bust he was pretty sure was buried under that stiff black cloth.

Maybe she'd guessed where his mind drifted, as her face colored and her eyes sharpened into narrow slits. "Your mother made sure all the trees were colored specifically for each room. The one in the living room, you'll be happy to know, is green." She averted her gaze and started yanking the ornaments off, pine needles dropping to the blood-red carpet, which was the only thing in this house he'd had a say in.

"So, Laura, is it?" Andy didn't know why, but there was something about this girl who'd been working in his household since the spring, when he'd first seen her cowering and petrified in the hallway the day Jed disappeared. His cousin, whom he loved dearly, was married to Diana, a woman who haunted his dreams but would never be his. Andy and Diana had worked together to find an injured Jed, thrown from the stallion he had been training up toward blue meadow, and Diana had added to the excitement by going into labor, delivering their baby boy, Danny, Andy's godson, that same night. He'd seen Laura in town shortly after holding a little boy's hand, and he'd since wondered who he was. She didn't look old enough to have children, as she appeared fresh out of high school. But, then again, he never asked, because he, unlike his father, didn't become personal with the staff, especially attractive young things who worked for him, because that wasn't okay. It was morally wrong, and he was having a hard time remembering what the other reason was. Ah, yes, sexual harassment.

"Yes?" The girl was staring at him with those big green eyes. He'd swear they were tinged with flecks of gold, which only illuminated her silky pale skin. She had not a spot of makeup on, but then, she didn't need it. She had soft skin that just begged to be touched, and, frankly, Andy was tired of all those women who caked on the pounds of makeup like a mask just to hop in their cars to go to the store.

"Sorry, been distracted lately. I was just wondering how things are going, if you're being treated okay. Do you like working here?"

Damn, that wasn't what he really wanted to know, but he had to remind himself again that she worked for him, for his family. As he thought about it, he didn't rightly know who had hired her, but the sizeable staff in the house and on the grounds was generally handled by Jules, the head housekeeper, a plump older lady who'd been with the family since Andy was in short pants. Andy wondered, too, if the deep lines on Jules' face and the thick gray in her hair were a result of him and the wily pranks he had played on her as a child.

Laura dropped her gaze again, her cheeks tinting a hint of pink as she boxed up the ornaments. "Everything's fine, sir." She said it so abruptly and carried on as if trying to ignore him, and that irritated the hell out of him. She worked for him. She'd damn well give him her full attention, and he'd see to that now.

"Laura, you work for me. So when I ask you something, I expect your attention and a truthful answer," he growled.

Her face colored a brighter red, and she glanced back at him warily. Andy, being as astute as he was, didn't miss the hint of dislike that she was doing her damnedest to hide, but it was a piss-poor attempt.

"You're right about one thing: I do work for you, but you don't own me, and you don't know me well enough to tell whether I gave you a truthful answer. So again, I'll repeat it, everything's fine, sir," she responded in a tone that was pure business. This time, she didn't look away as she continued to blush furiously, her lips pursed and trembling slightly as she stared up at him.

"If that's all, sir, I'll finish taking down these ornaments and haul the tree out of here." Again, she stared him down with those green eyes, resembling a very enticing witch, a witch he wouldn't mind getting to know a little better.

Andy uncrossed his arms and moved to his desk, pulling out his leather chair and sitting down. He propped both his booted feet on the sleek polished wood top of the desk, crossing his legs at the ankles, and watched her, lacing his fingers behind his head. She seemed startled, as her eyes widened. Maybe she expected him to leave.

"Carry on" was all he said.

She took a moment to collect herself before continuing to yank ornaments from the branches as if she were being timed. Pine needles flew everywhere. She was in a hurry, all right, not just to finish but to get the hell away from him.

When she bent over in that god-awful uniform, the dress rode up her thighs, and he was treated to a view of her shapely legs. She was tiny, her head wouldn't have topped his shoulders—and nervous as hell, too. He could see her trembling. Although not obvious, it was something he sensed, just like he sensed she wasn't thinking about the poor tree. She was just ripping those damn ornaments from that tacky tree as fast as she could, and he had no doubt she'd bolt as soon as the last one was off. For the life of him, he'd never experienced a woman running from him. This was intriguing, or it would have been if he didn't feel so irritated by the fact that it bothered him. Women didn't do that, not to Andy Friessen. Women found any ridiculous excuse to find a way to be around him. In town, at the store, dropping items, a purse, a bag—one woman even unbuttoned her blouse to expose a generous amount of indecent skin before crossing the street to him, putting an extra sway into each step. He'd never had a problem finding a woman for anything. The fact was that most of them bored him to tears, except Diana, his cousin's wife. And she'd never be his.

"Oh, no!"

Andy was so deep in thought, he only glimpsed Laura as she took a header into the white Christmas tree, and it came crashing down, all twelve feet of tinted fir needles, with a whoosh and scrape of wood. Something thumped hard, and glass shattered.

Andy jumped up, slamming his feet on the thick carpet as he raced around the desk. Laura was tangled in the tree. Her dress had ridden up, showing the elastic of her old-lady panties. The only thing Andy could think was what a waste they were on such a lovely round, curvy butt.

"Are you okay?" Andy reached down and lifted

Laura as he would a child, and he sat her on the edge of the desk.

"Mr. Friessen, whatever is going on in here?" Jules, the older, graying, plump housekeeper who ran the estate, hurried into the library but was stopped by the downed tree. She slapped both hands to her round cheeks and shrieked. Shattered ornaments, bits of fir needles, and broken branches were strewn across the plush red carpet and the sofa table. The huge tree had knocked over one of the leather chairs and the bar that had been moved to the other side of the room to make room for it. Decanters and liquor bottles lay on their sides, the crystal shattered, liquor pooling and seeping into the carpet. Laura sat perched on the edge of Andy's desk, white fir needles sticking out of her blond hair, though they were hard to see unless he really looked. Her neat bun had drooped, and her hair hung in an untidy mess. Her entire expression had turned into that of a lost young girl, as if she couldn't believe what she'd done.

"Oh my God!" Caroline, his mother, shouted as she strode in with all the elegance of a queen, dressed in a deep green silk knee-length dress that hugged her every curve and showed what an attractive woman she still was. Her shoulder-length light hair was impeccably groomed, and when she stopped beside Jules, her mouth opened as if she couldn't think of what to say. Then her shrewd gaze landed on Laura, and her pale blue eyes turned frosty and unforgiving. "What a mess you've made, girl."

Even Andy was taken aback by the iciness of her tone, and he didn't miss the way Laura cringed, like a dowdy school girl. Hell, Andy had cowered under his mother as a little boy when she'd have one of her tantrums, generally after he'd broken some useless and really expensive trinket of hers.

"I'm so sorry, ma'am. I tripped, but I'll… c-clean this up," she stuttered and pressed her small hand to her throat.

Andy narrowed his eyes and watched Caroline, as she appeared to just be winding up for one of her many tantrums. As far back as Andy could remember, his mother had never shown an ounce of empathy toward anyone, not even her own child. And this time was no different. She glared at Laura with as much feeling as a viper and the energy of one that was about to strike, and then she surveyed the damage, the disarray, and the mess with a swift, well-organized glance. Lifting her chin and straightening her back, she spoke clearly: "The damage will come out of your last check. Jules, see that she's escorted off the property within the next five minutes." She looked over to Laura. "Do not ever return. If you do, the proper authorities will be called."

Andy jerked his gaze from his mother to Laura's wide eyes, now filled with tears. He could tell she was struggling to hold it together, as she appeared to have trouble swallowing. "Mother, it was an accident. You're being a bit hasty. For God's sake, it's just a stupid tree, and I ordered her to get it out of here. I made it clear to you before that if you want to decorate the rest of the house, it's fine—just stay out of my office," Andy said to his mother, but Caroline, who could be so prickly at times, stood unbending and in fact raised one eyebrow.

"Anderson, the tree stays. The girl goes. I have guests arriving for our annual Christmas party. You'll have your office back after Christmas. Jules, the girl, get rid of her." She literally snapped her fingers, and Jules jumped, saying, "Yes, Mrs. Friessen," and motioning frantically at Laura.

Caroline didn't stay but strode from the room, the heels of her silver pumps clicking across the marble floor of the grand entry and down two steps to an exquisite living room, with fancy white trim, which was decorated in peach and gold, floor-to-ceiling windows, and velvety white carpet. A twelve-foot cream-colored Christmas tree was also decorated to perfection with gold, silver, and red.

Caroline walked as if she were in a beauty contest, head high, striding to a small round dinette set where one of the maids had set a china tea service. Caroline had to know he was following her, but she ignored Andy, which was a skill she'd perfected years before. It was amazing—his mother broke the mold in snobbery, and he'd never met anyone who could look right through him and choose whether to see him quite like his mother could.

She brushed aside the white napkin that had been folded over the gold china cup, pouring tea and adding a generous amount of milk. She sipped and picked up the day timer sitting on the antique glass-top desk by the window. She never glanced up as she sat in the white leather chair that was matched to all the furnishings in the room. "Is there something you would like, Andy? As I said, I have a million things to do today to organize this household and be ready in time for the party." She glanced up at him and pasted on one of her practiced smiles that always charmed the senators.

"Mother, I am not going to continue butting heads with you. What you did, firing Laura just now, wasn't okay. For God's sake, she didn't deserve to be treated like that," Andy stated, rather annoyed, and gestured toward the library before setting his hands on his hips. He stood in front of her desk, glaring down at her until she slowly, with the control of a seasoned politician, set down her tea and folded her hands neatly on the desk, eyeing him coolly.

"Anderson, this is my house. Therefore, the servants work for me, and I will decide how they are treated and who stays and who goes, not you." She picked up her cup again and sipped, then gave him one of her disapproving looks. "Laura, really? Already on a first-name basis? In some ways, you really are like your father." She said it with such disdain, and the fact that she had alluded to the possibility of him playing hanky-panky with the maid irritated the hell out of him, even though, less than ten minutes before, he had been imagining Laura dressed down in something completely indecent and doing all kinds of lewd things with him. He often wondered what kind of sixth sense his mother had for the perverse. But then, she had to, being married to his dad, Todd, who had the uncanny ability to sniff out a new mistress as soon as he tired of one, just to keep his interests alive and his bed warm. His father could be like a hound dog when he was hot on the trail of a new scent. Andy liked to think that trait was Todd's alone, and he would ram his fist in the face of anyone who accused him of being a scoundrel, toying with women's hearts and tossing them away when he was done. There was a very big difference between Andy having any woman he wanted and Andy being like Todd Friessen.

So he bared his teeth and growled at his mother, because he was damn tired of cleaning up after his father and putting up with his mother's arrogance. "You know what's absolutely amazing? How you treat people and have for years, just by snapping your fingers and expecting everyone to jump, with no care to anyone's feelings. You and Dad are so much the same, it's absolutely terrifying."

"I am not like that…" Caroline sputtered, but Andy didn't let her finish.

"You are exactly like him. You believe everyone is replaceable and have little care for anyone's feelings. Dad, with every woman he beds. You, with the servants, how you treat everyone. You know what? I'm done cleaning up. I've got my own life to live." Andy was shouting, but Caroline hardened her expression better than any snake he'd ever met. When she did that, even Andy felt a rush of worry, because the woman was the only one who could yank the rug out from under him— there was no way to know what she was thinking.

"I've invited Alexis Johnston. You remember, the senator's daughter. She just graduated from Stanton, and I told the senator that you'd be her escort for the party. He's counting on you. Don't disappoint me, Andy. Whatever you're doing with your maids, keep it in the closet, where it belongs." She issued the order as if she expected him to fall into line, then picked up a stack of envelopes and started filing through them.

Andy laughed so hard that tears came to his eyes. His mother really was a piece of work. "You must have been drinking or something, because you don't ever order me to do anything. You certainly are not fixing me up with any woman." He ground his teeth together before growling, "Not ever, Mother." He could feel the irritation biting the back of his neck as he strode out, and he wanted nothing more than to ram his fist into a wall.

But he didn't, and he wasn't even out of the room when Caroline spoke in a loud, clear voice: "Oh, I think you will, since Senator Johnson is on the very committee that your cousin Jed approached for funding for his therapeutic riding."

Andy's blood chilled, and all the fiery anger he had been containing moments ago was replaced with an array of worry he hadn't experienced in a long time. Only his mother could knock him over and leave him absolutely speechless. He turned slowly to meet the sharp gleam in the woman's ice-blue eyes. A woman who had given birth to him, a woman he had no doubt would sell him down the river for the right offer if it was in her best interest.

"Yes, the senator and I had quite a chat about how tight funding is now, with the national debt this country carries and how selective any new programming must be. It's quite a project, really, that your cousin is starting with that Claremont he married. I mean, really, the senator can't be providing funding to just anyone." Her face was hard as stone, not a flicker of emotion. He wondered for a moment if she had a bone of feeling in her body.

"Diana is her name, and she was a Fulton when she married Jed. She never deserved to be treated that way as a child. Diana and Jed are good people, Mother. You stay away from them, and stay out of Jed's business." He ground out each word, reminding himself she was his mother and, no matter what, it was never okay to strangle one's own mother. But he also knew his mother never made threats; she insinuated, she dug, and she destroyed those she didn't like, and she never gave any warning. *The Art of War*, she could have written it. But Caroline, being Caroline, always had an agenda, and it was never wise to let her know what mattered to him, because she would use it. Andy had learned that the hard way over the years. When he was twelve, she'd gotten rid of his pony, Chantelle, the one he'd whispered all his dreams to. Just because he refused to go to some fancy boys' school in England that her father, uncles, and brothers had all attended.

"I told the senator you'll pick up his daughter when she flies in tomorrow. She'll be staying here at the estate."

This time, Andy walked away before he could respond, the fury pouring out of him with each step. Back in the library, two servants were righting the downed Christmas tree, and another scrawny maid in a sack-like dress was on her knees, cleaning up the shattered glass and decanters. Another one was scrubbing the liquor seeping into the carpet.

"Get out!" Andy roared, and each of them stopped what they were doing and left.

Andy was breathing hard as if he'd run across the estate. He jammed his fingers in his hair as he paced and froze in front of the large window, watching as Laura was escorted down the front driveway.

"Lorhainne Eckhart is one of my go to authors when I want a guaranteed good book. So many twists and turns, but also so much love and such a strong sense of family."

(LORA W., REVIEWER)

New York Times & USA Today bestseller Lorhainne Eckhart is best known for writing Raw Relatable Real Romance where "Morals and family are running themes." As one fan calls her, she is the "Queen of the family saga." (aherman) writing "the ups and downs of what goes on within a family but also with some suspense, angst and of course a bit of romance thrown in for good measure." Follow Lorhainne on Bookbub to receive alerts on New Releases and Sales and join her mailing list at LorhainneEckhart.com for her Monday Blog, all book news, giveaways and FREE reads. With over 120 books, audiobooks, and multiple series published and available at all, retailers now translated into six languages. She is a multiple recipient of the Readers' Favorite Award for Suspense and Romance, and lives in the Pacific Northwest on an island, is the mother of three, her oldest has autism and she is an advocate for never giving up on your dreams.

"Lorhainne Eckhart has this uncanny way of just hitting the spot every time with her books."

(CAROLINE L., REVIEWER)

The O'Connells: *The O'Connells of Livingston, Montana are not your typical family. A riveting collection of stories surrounding the ups and downs of what goes on within a family but also with some suspense, angst and of course a bit of romance thrown in for good measure. "I thought I loved the Friessens, but I absolutely adore the O'Connell's. Each and every book has different genres of stories, but the one thing in common is how she is able to wrap it around the family, which is the heart of each story." (C. Logue)*

The Friessens: *An emotional big family*

romance series, the Friessen family siblings find their relationships tested, lay their hearts on the line, and discover lasting love! "Lorhainne Eckhart is one of my go to authors when I want a guaranteed good book. So many twists and turns, but also so much love and such a strong sense of family." (Lora W., Reviewer)

The Parker Sisters: *The Parker Sisters are a close-knit family, and like any other family they have their ups and downs. Eckhart has crafted another intense family drama… "The character development is outstanding, and the emotional investment is high…" (Aherman, Reviewer)*

The McCabe Brothers: *Join the five McCabe siblings on their journeys to the dark and dangerous side of love! An intense, exhilarating collection of romantic thrillers you won't want to miss. — "Eckhart has a new series that is definitely worth the read. The queen of the family saga started this series with a spin-off of her wildly successful Friessen series." From a Readers' Favorite award—winning author and "queen of the family saga" (Aherman)*

Billy Jo McCabe Mystery: *The social worker and the cop, an unlikely couple drawn together on a small, secluded Pacific Northwest island where nothing is as it* *seems. Protecting the innocent comes at a cost, and what seems to be a sleepy, quiet town is anything but.*

Lorhainne loves to hear from her readers! You can connect with me at:

www.LorhainneEckhart.com
lorhainneeckhart.le@gmail.com

In the Family
In the Silence
In the Charm
Unexpected Consequences
It Was Always You
The First Time I Saw You
Welcome to My Arms
Welcome to Boston
I'll Always Love You
Ground Rules
A Reason to Breathe
You Are My Everything
Anything For You
The Homecoming
Stay Away From My Daughter
The Bad Boy
A Place of Our Own
The Visitor
All About Devon
Long Past Dawn
How to Heal a Heart
Keep Me In Your Heart

The O'Connells
The Neighbor
The Third Call
The Secret Husband
The Quiet Day
The Commitment
The Missing Father
The Hometown Hero
Justice
The Family Secret

The Fallen O'Connell
The Return of the O'Connells
And The She Was Gone
The Stalker
The O'Connell Family Christmas
The Girl Next Door
Broken Promises
The Gatekeeper
The Hunted

The McCabe Brothers
Don't Stop Me (Vic)
Don't Catch Me (Chase)
Don't Run From Me (Aaron)
Don't Hide From Me (Luc)
Don't Leave Me (Claudia)
Out of Time

A Billy Jo McCabe Mystery
Nothing As it Seems
Hiding in Plain Sight
The Cold Case
The Trap
Above the Law
The Stranger at the Door
The Children
The Last Stand
The Charity
The Sacrifice

The Street Fighter
Finding Home

The Wilde Brothers
The One (Joe and Margaret)
The Honeymoon, A Wilde Brothers Short
Friendly Fire (Logan and Julia)
Not Quite Married, A Wilde Brothers Short
A Matter of Trust (Ben and Carrie)
The Reckoning, A Wilde Brothers Christmas
Traded (Jake)
Unforgiven (Samuel)
The Holiday Bride

Married in Montana
His Promise
Love's Promise
A Promise of Forever

The Parker Sisters
Thrill of the Chase
The Dating Game
Play Hard to Get
What We Can't Have
Go Your Own Way
A June Wedding

Kate & Walker
One Night
Edge of Night
Last Night

Walk the Right Road Series
The Choice
Lost and Found
Merkaba

Bounty
Blown Away: The Final Chapter
He Came Back

The Saved Series
Saved
Vanished
Captured

Single Titles
Loving Christine